Diatomaceous Earth

Diatomaceous Earth

OR

THE HUMDRUM LIFE OF THE LACKADAISICAL BARRY:

A FIELD GUIDE FOR THE BIRDS

H. Williams

Perry Wynkle Publishing
Boston

Who's the cat's father?

Library of Congress Control Number: 2016949476
ISBN-13: 9780997841602
ISBN-10: 0997841605
Perry Wynkle Publishing

Cover photo by H. Williams
Cover design by P. Orzech
Kayak photo by L. Caron
Interior illustration by D. Luther

October 2016
Perry Wynkle Publishing, Boston, MA
PerryWynklePublishing@gmail.com

The following
combination of words was
discovered at a highway rest area,
affectionately termed the "Pickle Park" by
local inhabitants. The individual who unearthed this
peculiar and convoluted manuscript claimed it was found
inside a "large, rusty-green" waste barrel. Purportedly,
it was somehow spotted underneath "three or four
banana peels," a broken Engelbert Humperdinck
album (Hansel and Gretel), and the letter
Q volume of the Encyclopedia
Britannica.

Note: Some say "Who's the cat's father?" was scrawled in
"chicken scratch" on a post-it note stuck to the front page
of this manuscript. They say the phrase has meaning, but
aren't sure what that meaning is.

Others maintain the handwriting on that note was nothing
more than illegible nonsense.

A third group claims the writing could be read, but was,
ultimately, infantile and inconsequential.

"My husband is the famous neuroscientist-turned-President of Marketing for Mersharty-Quill Tizzy. He's the co-inventor of the revolutionary drug Trans-Baux: 'The Medication For When You're Between Medications.' No doubt you've heard of him."

-PRISCILLA DRINKWATER

A Great Coincidence?

———•———

IT WAS THE TAIL-END OF a topsy-turvy, hot and hazy summer when I spied the last few words of Wayne's clandestine, pay-phone pow-wow.

The situation unfolded as follows:

The gas pumps and parking lot at the New World Convenience Store were devoid of patrons when I arrived. Alas, when I exited the mini-mart, I saw that Wayne had magically materialized at a pay phone next to the ice boxes. This was odd. I could have sworn I saw him ten minutes prior, loitering by the gates of Needles Cemetery. How he tele-ported from there to a call box so damned quickly is truly a mystery.

Never-the-less, there he was with the receiver held tightly to his face and a red box of Captain Crunch at his feet. The phone was pressed between his right shoulder and cheek and his hands were cupped over his mouth. It was evident that he didn't want any of his words to be released into the atmosphere. It was also abundantly clear he had no idea how to appear innocent and inconspicuous.

I knew I had a once in a lifetime opportunity before me. Finally, I had the chance to get a rare look into the inner-world of Wayne. He was trying so hard to look like a spy, and was so engrossed in his conversation, he didn't notice me when I casually walked up behind him. The irony of the situation almost made me laugh.

He did all of the loud, but muffled talking.

"Okay, okay Dr. Billi... – I mean, Seafood Stu," he said. "I'll pay in cash! Just make sure you don't forget those records and x-rays again. Remember, I will come up to you and say:

Business in the front!

You will reply,

Pahrty in the back!

And then we exchange. It's as simple as that. Let's just hope the natives are friendlier this time."

He hung up the phone.

Initially, I wanted to scare the shit out of him, yell something behind his back, and make him jump out of his skin. Instead, I decided to wait and see how long it would take him to detect me.

He didn't.

He picked up his box of Captain Crunch and walked away.

I followed.

The Fountain of Life

———•———

WAYNE MEANDERED. EVENTUALLY, I REASONED he was taking a rather roundabout way home. Then, I figured he was probably concerned someone was following him. Just as that thought dawned upon me, however, I witnessed something quite out-of-the-ordinary.

While Wayne walked briskly down the sidewalk and munched upon Horatio Magellan's sweetened corn and oats, a monstrously sized man – dressed completely in brown – rushed out from behind a block of arborvitaes. In one fell swoop he punched Wayne right-square in the face. A surprise attack. He then added an assault to his battery.

"Now we're even, bitch!" he said gruffly.

Wayne looked at his assailant in a dejected sort of way. He obviously knew him. And somehow - despite the fact that he was holding his head down in shame - I heard him shakily respond.

"Yeah, I guess you're right," he murmured.

And with that, the brown crusader shook his head in pity and took off across the street. Wayne stood still for a moment and rubbed his damaged, swelling face. He turned around, almost saw me crouched behind a mail-box, and ate another handful of Captain Crunch. He then continued on his way.

When he was close to his street, he cut through his neighbor's backyard – a Mr. Appleton, I believe – and stopped in front of a tacky-elaborate water fountain. It was a pretty nice one - as far as garden oases go - complete with two levels and a good size reservoir at its base. It also included three plastic squirrels that, due to hydro-power, whirled like dervishes.

Wayne gazed upon the fountain in an extra-special type of transcendental stupor. It must have been the flowing water that caught his attention and transfixed him. It never took much to mesmerize his brain.

He stood there and watched the liquid circulate and the squirrels gyrate for an abnormal amount of time. In fact, he was there for so long, maybe five minutes or so, I began to worry Appleton would spot him. To save my mind from the stress and tension, I considered revealing myself and physically removing Wayne from the property. But, precisely when I decided to take action, Wayne caught me off-guard. Abruptly, his hands traveled down to his crotch and he calmly unzipped his pants. Unfettered, he relieved himself into the base of the fountain.

As soon as he finished adding to the water level, he ran away laughing like a weasel. Before I knew it, he had jumped over some shrubbery, a rusty upside down fence, and vanished into his barren, neglected backyard.

"Many people mistakenly pronounce
cumberbund as cummerbund."

"I have a feeling these people are the same as those
who misspell cumberbund as cummerbund."

-WAYNE

CHAPTER 2A

Dr. and Mrs. Drinkwater

———◆———

AFTER I GOT MY DOSE of Wayne and his idiosyncrasies, I decided to head on home. I wanted some time to relax and float aimlessly in the pool. Before I got there, however, I opted to check in on my parents. I wasn't necessarily concerned about them - I just wanted to know if the status quo was still firmly in place. Both of their cars were in the garage, so I knew they had to be somewhere in the house.

I came across my mother first - at least, I somewhat did. She was upstairs, and by the sound of it, she was in her office, feverishly plugging away at her keyboard. The door was shut and had a sign on it that said "Do Not Disturb When Door is Closed: Writing in Progress." She takes that sign pretty seriously, so I didn't disrupt her. She was probably working on Small Sacrifices, her advice and etiquette column that appears weekly in *The Needles News Tribune*.

After I was stymied by signage, I headed to my father's office in the basement. As I descended the steps, I could hear what sounded like a re-run of *Family Feud* playing loudly on the television. My father - who didn't hear me come down the stairs - was sitting at his desk in a brown, leather, wing chair with gold-studded arms. On the wall behind him were his framed degrees and a signed, glossy photo of Robert Urich, taken during his *Spenser: For Hire* days. There was also a certificate next to his Ph.D diploma, which verified the thread count of his Egyptian cotton, 1,001 Arabian Nights bed sheets.

I don't think he saw me at first - despite the fact that I stood a mere five or so feet away from him. He was looking toward the television, but I'm not so sure he was tuned into the program. He was in one of his zones and his eyes were set in a vacant, dead stare. I gave him an extra minute or two to snap out of it, and, luckily, he did.

He wasn't surprised to see me.

"Ah, Barry, good to see you," he said indifferently. "I've been meaning to talk to you about the pool. It appears as though the deep end is a tad murky. We don't want that green algae to spiral out of control. You know what I mean?"

I responded instantly with some exaggerated enthusiasm.

"Absolutely!" I said. "We can't have that. Not in our pool!"

He perked up after he heard my response. I could tell that he was happy our united front against algae sounded strong and everlasting. I guess he wasn't able to tell I was a touch insincere.

He continued his directives with more confidence.

"You probably need to drop some of those chlorine bombs in there, you know? That should be done at *least* once a week. *At least.* Also, make sure to refill that floating chlorinator. It runs out before you know it!"

I maintained my pseudo-eagerness and assured him I would do as instructed.

"Will do," I said. "I'll get right on it. Anything else before I skedaddle and hop to everything?"

He put the fingertips of his right hand to his neck and squinted his eyes. I'm sure he wanted to make it look like he was thinking - a conscious or unconscious action – even though he already knew what he was going to say.

"Well," he continued, "to be perfectly honest, I have a feeling the pH may be a little high for my taste. Looks kind of cloudy - if you know what I mean. See if you can get some pH reducer in there. Use the jets to help spread it around, okay? We want that pH at 7.4. No more, no less. That's our goal. 7.4."

"Okay, I'm on it," I said. "Thanks for the tips!"

I turned around and headed up the stairs. When I got to the top, he dispensed some last minute aquatic chemistry advice.

"You may want to backwash and clean the filter as well," he yelled. "Add some new diatomaceous earth. And don't forget to brush, skim, and vacuum! Brush-skim-vac!"

I told him I would and he, almost simultaneously, raised the volume on the television.

"Humankind's greatest accomplishment?
Well, I guess if I had to choose one thing, it
would be that we've done an impeccable job
soiling a previously beautiful world."

-DR. DRINKWATER

CHAPTER 2 B

The Attractive Nuisance

———

IT WAS ALREADY 6:00 P.M., but still hot and sunny when I arrived at the pool. I meant to attend to the algae and pH right away, but I was distracted by the diving board. Before long, I was at the end of it, tempting fate - extended over the water as far as possible. I inspected the clouds as they passed overhead and watched the sunlight dance around in the pool. I'm no entomologist, but I'm pretty sure I could hear some crickets, cicadas, and katydids, making whatever noises they like to create. I know for certain, however, some squirrels and other wildlife were shitting around and causing a ruckus in the bushes.

Although it felt good to stand at the tip of the diving board and collect my thoughts, I eventually relocated to my reliable rubber raft - the HMS Talbot. Without getting wet, I carefully climbed in the vessel and pushed myself off the side, straight toward the deep end.

While I floated, I considered my father's water treatment instructions. I also wondered why he's so preoccupied with water maintenance. Thing is, I'm the only one who uses the pool. I don't think he's ever stepped foot in it, and my mother hasn't thrown one of her pool parties in ages. On top of that, my younger brother, Gary-Spelled-Like-Gerry, refuses to get too close to the water. He's afraid someone will toss him in and watch him drown - one of those self-fulfilling prophecies that's just waiting to happen. He's ten or eleven now - at least I think so - and he's never learned how to swim.

Every time I climb aboard the HMS Talbot I think of the day it was presented to me - along with Barrie. It was my birthday, I must have been about six, and my parents were waiting for me by the stairs at the shallow end of the pool. At first, I thought the two of them were up to something sinister - maybe some kind of sacrificial ritual - but then they said "Happy birthday," parted to each side, and revealed my new inflatable yellow raft.

"Barry, this is your private, luxury yacht," my mother proclaimed. "We've named it The HMS Talbot."

"Proportionately," my father added, "given the size of the pool and this vessel, I'd say it's among the biggest in the world - at least three hundred feet. A fine craft for a fine man who wants to make a big impression on the world."

I can't remember what I said in response. I probably said nothing or "Thank you."

I do remember, though, that my father's demeanor suddenly shifted from playful to gravely serious. He leaned in close to me and whispered into my ear.

"Remember, Barry," he said, "a person doesn't come by an opportunity like this often - if ever. You must take good care of the HMS Talbot and treat it the way it will treat you."

I nodded and accepted my responsibilities.

Fortunately, my mother interjected and ended the solemn moment.

"Now, Barry, it's time to christen the HMS Talbot," she instructed. "Take this can of A&W Root Beer, shake it as much as you can, and anoint the Talbot with fizz."

She handed me the can of soda and I did as I was told. After the baptism, my parents provided a round of applause.

Mission accomplished.

"It's official!" my father said. "All that's left for you to do is climb aboard and leisurely sail toward the deep."

Again, I did as I was told. That particular assignment appealed to me.

CHAPTER 3

Barrie: An Introduction

———•———

NEXT THING I KNEW, I was fast asleep in the deep end. I guess there's something about drifting there that knocks me out every time. One second I was surrounded by my family near the stairs. The next, I was in the land of Nod, napping in the HMS Talbot at the other end of the pool.

I'm not sure how long I was unconscious in the raft. All I know is that my father was hovering over me when I woke up. He had an oar in his hand and was gently tapping me on the shoulder with it.

"Looks like you fell asleep at the helm, Barry," he said when he realized I was awake. "Luckily, you didn't run aground. Good thing there were no passengers on board."

I was still rather groggy and shook my head up and down without thinking over his observation.

He handed me the oar and I pulled myself up as best I could.

"There's something else," he continued, "I need to show you in the basement - for your birthday. A bonus gift, you might say.

How about you take your time, disembark, and join me downstairs in a couple of minutes?"

He quietly walked away, opened the pool gate, closed it, and was gone. I dipped my hands into the water to help me wake up, and paddled to the stairs in the shallow end.

In less than three minutes I was at my father's office, staring in awe at a hefty-looking gift-wrapped box on his desk. He was behind it, but all I could see was his head and the blank, yet all-knowing, expression on his face.

My father recognized my curiosity was piqued and skillfully chimed in with some directions.

"You see this big box, Barry-boy? It's your final birthday present. Why don't you climb up on this chair here and carefully unwrap it?"

I climbed up as suggested and ripped the paper on that box to shreds. I think my father was caught slightly off-guard when he saw how fast I completed the task. I suppose rapidly removing gift paper is one of my many insignificant talents.

What I uncovered, however, left me puzzled, numb, and speechless.

Sitting inside the cardboard box, trapped behind some shiny plastic, was a miniature facsimile of me. The two-foot-tall doll was dressed in brown overalls, a blue paisley shirt, and a matching pair of white and blue saddle shoes. His hair and eyes were the same colors as mine, and his nose, mouth, and ears were spot on as well. The name of the doll, Barrie, was located at the top of the box in purple bubble letters. There was a rainbow beneath the name Barrie and an exclamation point after it.

My father took note of my perplexed reaction.

"You're getting up there in age, Barry," he said. "And the truth is, I can't be there for you all the time. I've got things to do. You've got things to do. Everybody's got things to do. So, you need to start relying on yourself. And Barrie here, well, he's going to help you think for yourself. Consider him a good friend. Someone who understands. Someone who wants to sift through your thoughts and feelings."

He waited for some type of response, but I said nothing. He carried on with his explanation.

"I just happened to be at that gigantic toy store, walking down a brightly lit aisle, searching for the perfect gift for you. That's when I first saw Barrie. He was in his box - just like he is now - only there were hundreds of him on each side of me. They were stacked on top of each other, as far as I could see. I couldn't believe it and I said to myself, 'That's it. It's meant to be. A Barrie for my Barry, a friend for him forever.' So, I grabbed one, and went straight to the register."

I was still at a loss for words. My father looked at me and waited for me to say something. I didn't.

To fill the gap, he opened the lid of the box and smoothly lifted Barrie out of his incarceration. I felt unnerved that he was set loose so quickly, that his emancipation came so easily. I didn't like the idea of him sharing the stuffy basement air with us. What's more, he was perfectly innocent looking - and, because of that, he looked perfectly evil.

My father could tell that I was caught off guard, so he tried to combat my ignorance of the doll with knowledge and answers to Barrie's many mysteries.

He stared at me intently. Then, he spoke to me in the same tone he used when he whispered in my ear at the pool.

"Now the thing is," he said, "Barrie here doesn't talk, you know? He does something much more important than talking."

He picked Barrie up with his left hand, pointed at him with his right, and stated:

"He listens."

He paused for a moment and gauged my reaction.

"So let me show you how he works, okay?" he continued. "Whenever you feel like you need to talk to me, or someone else, I want you to take Barrie and push the green button in his back. Just like this."

He flipped Barrie so he was face down on the desk, lifted a flap in his overalls, and pushed a green button. It all seemed kind of gruesome to me. It looked like a mini version of myself was undergoing surgery on an operation table.

"Now that we've hit the green button," he went on, "all that's left to do is talk to your buddy Barrie. Tell him whatever's on your mind, whatever's bothering you. Whatever you think he needs to know. Just make sure to speak on the slow-side, loudly, and clearly. When you're done talking, push this red button, like this, and Barrie will know you've finished sharing your thoughts with him."

He pushed the red button and Barrie officially entered my world.

"You mean to tell me the thyroid is in your neck and not the ass? Go fuck yourself, Barry. I'm not that fucking stupid."

-WAYNE

CHAPTER 4

One of Three

———◆———

It's PERFECTLY QUIET IN THE gloomy nocturnal air. A bleak wind chills my skin and my breath appears before me. It must be autumn. I can see myself, and I'm alone and walking aimlessly, haunting a cold hill's side. My face is paler than usual and adorned with a haggard, woebegone look – the result of I am not sure what. Since it seems to be the only direction to go, I slowly make my way to the hilltop. As I walk, my feet encounter more and more leaves that quietly rest upon the ground. Despite the lack of light, I can tell most have already changed to shades of rusty orange, brown and amber. They're slowly decomposing, returning to the Earth. Although some have a little life left to them, most have succumbed to the elements, dried out, and shriveled. I picture a vampire sucking the blood out of their veins. He cleans his fangs with his sleeve and vanishes into thin air.

I look up and see a monstrously sized oak tree - presumably the tree the fallen leaves once called home - and sluggishly meander toward it. Then, in mere seconds, I find myself standing at the top of the hill, beneath the gnarled behemoth I spied. I wonder how I've appeared underneath it so quickly, but that fleeting thought is soon misplaced and forgotten. Instead, I find myself marveling at the tree's limbs - limbs that stretch out over an improbable lake's black, murky water. The tarn is saturated with leaves. Those that fell most recently float silently in place on the glassy surface. Older decayed leaves, those that quietly drowned, lie beneath them. I switch my gaze from the water and scan the withered sedge that surrounds the pool. My eyes see movement, I squint, and I discover I'm not alone.

On the opposite side of the pond are two figures, one larger than the other, standing ten-or-so paces apart. Although it's still quite dark, I can see them well enough, and realize they're engaged in a game of catch. The big one throws to the small one. The small one throws to the big one. I walk toward the two. Closer now, I can tell they're both males, probably father and son. The father throws to the son. I walk toward the two. I'm only fifty feet away, and it dawns on me the pair haven't said a word to one another. They've been playing in total silence, without expression. The son throws to the father. The father throws to the son. This time, though, the son fumbles. The pattern breaks. The ball, in what looks like slow motion, rolls - lazily, haphazardly - and tumbles into the water.

Next thing I know, I'm waist deep in near freezing water. It's piercing cold, as if I'm trapped in the middle of an ice-box. Although I can't see them, I know the father and son are still behind me. I can feel their beady eyes on my back, indifferently watching me as I retrieve their ball. It isn't far from me, though - it floats just outside the reach of my right arm. I extend myself farther, and as a result, I lose my footing. The frigid water rises to my chest, but I'm close enough to collect the ball. I extend my arm, grab it, and hold it firmly in hand. I turn, raise my arm above water, and toss the ball toward its owners.

The father and son make no attempt to catch it. The ball lands beyond them, bounces, and rolls off into the night. The two of them stare at me blankly and show no sign of gratitude. A wall of silence separates us - a wall I'm hesitant to break. Instead, my concern turns to the water. It's time for me to get out. My body is too cold.

I make my way to the edge and discover that it's steep - much steeper than I thought. I try to climb free, but I fall backwards. One failed attempt follows another until the cold water deviously, but gently, lulls me to sleep. A sinister fever sets in and assumes control. I look down at the palms of my hands and see that they're larger than normal and deathly-pale. Immediately, I look up at the father and son and discover they're retreating. I watch them as they walk, side-by-side, and slowly disappear into the fog. From far above, I can see my small figure standing in the dark water. My lips are purple and blue, my mouth agape.

CHAPTER 5

Messages in a Balloon?

———•———

IT WAS DUSK WHEN I woke up. Something in the bushes was scurrying about and snatched me from my slumber. Unfortunately, my eyes couldn't adjust in time to catch the culprit. Whoever - whatever it was - disappeared too fast. As I grew accustomed to the early evening gloom, however, I was distracted by something else entirely. It was directly above me in the sky, descending toward my coordinates. It looked like some kind of meteor or flying saucer.

Initially, I was concerned it would crash land on me and my raft - obliterate us completely. I probably should have taken cover, but I assumed my efforts would be futile. Then, luckily, I realized whatever was dropping toward me wasn't a threat at all.

It was merely a dying, red, latex balloon.

I don't know how a person could arrange for a deflated dirigible to touch down precisely onto my lap, but that's what happened. I inspected it as soon as it arrived, and I could tell something was inside of it. I pulled the poor thing apart and discovered three pieces of paper. Fortunately, there was enough light left to read them.

Each clipping was a different size and cut from a newspaper, most likely *The Needles News Tribune*. The first one I read was a job posting. It said the following:

Courtroom Abstract Artist Needed:
Salary Commensurate With Experience
Applicants: Please Call 978-555-9597
Offered Via Mirro Enterprises
411 Elm Street, Needles, MA.

The second clipping was about a man who was killed by a grizzly bear. Some of it was missing:

BEAR ATTACKS AND KILLS TRAINER
Authorities puzzled, uncertain if bear will be killed in retribution.

Horribilis the XVI showed no signs of violence before the attack. Although, as several wild-life experts have noted, he was, after all, a grizzly bear. The victim's name has yet to be released. Friends, neighbors, and colleagues are still trying to make sense of the bloody assault that onlookers say lasted at least fifteen minutes. Grief counselors will be...

The third clipping was an advertisement for a cottage for rent. It was completely intact and said the following:

Guest Cottage for Rent

Lovely guest cottage available for selected nights of the week to a normal male commuter who requires local accommodations. I will be in the main house the nights you are here. Not available Tuesdays, Wednesdays from 1-3 p.m., and Fridays. Those days I intend to occupy the room. We will use the same bed.

The cottage is free from cigarette smoke, marijuana smoke, alcohol, dander, harsh chemicals, rap music, and certain perfumes (a list will be provided).

Shower use is permitted, but only if swimming trunks are worn whilst cleansing.

Please, no additional friends are allowed.

The per night cost is $50.00, plus your share of the utilities. Optional use of the wood burning stove to lower the amount you pay. A deduction in rent will be provided to someone who cleans and re-points the chimney.

$265.00 deposit and four references required (from non-relatives only and at least one supervisor).

After I read the balloon's contents - which made little sense to me - I decided it was time to exit the pool. I sailed toward the ladder in the corner and painstakingly extricated myself from the HMS Talbot. It's never easy transferring to solid ground, but I did so successfully, without getting any water on my suit. Thing is, I was so wrapped up in the process, my brother was able to get the jump on me - something he is wont to do. His quivering voice emanated from behind-below and called out my name, as if he didn't know it belonged to me.

"Barry?" Gary-Spelled-Like-Gerry inquired.

He startled me, but I knew it was him almost instantly. I turned around - calmly and coolly. I didn't want the angelic pee-wee to think he could get the best of me so easily.

I affirmed that I was, in fact, myself.

"Yes, Gary-Spelled-Like-Gerry," I said. "You've identified me correctly."

He didn't respond.

He stood there and bit his lip, head down, fidgeting with his hands.

"Well," I said, "what can I do for you?"

He answered timidly in his extra-innocent voice. He was trying his best to look like he was about to cry.

"I was just wah-wah-wondering, Ba-Barry. I was just wondering about ra-ra-rocks and what they do-do all day. Are they ah-ah-live? And what about i-i-islands? How do they stay in one pa-pah-place, not fa-fa-float away in the oh-sha-sha-en?"

I was in no mood for this type of behavior and I let him know.

"Listen, Gary-Spelled-Like-Gerry, I'm not falling for your *Leave it to Beaver* bullshit. And stop that adorable stuttering act. Everyone knows you're faking it."

"Bah-bah-but I just..."

"What did I just say, Gary-Spelled-Like-Gerry?" I interrupted. "What did I just say? I'm not a violent person, but if you continue this ruse, I'm going to throw you into the pool. Do you understand? I'm going to pick you up over my head and toss you right the fuck into the pool."

The thought of being launched into the pool was enough to frighten Gary-Spelled-Like-Gerry away immediately. He booked it toward the gate, opened it, and dashed through within seconds. He moved so fast, it looked like he was in one of those time-lapse videos.

After he rapidly departed, I followed his delicate footsteps and closed the gate properly behind him. The ugly truth is Gary-Spelled-Like-Gerry has never understood the importance of closing what he's opened, picking up after himself, pushing in chairs, and other simple tasks that require minimal effort.

Anyhow, I went through the motions of closing the gate and started to feel sleepy again. In my defense, it was an unusual day - mentally taxing - and my mind must have known it was time to retire. Then again, as my hand left the closed gate, I remember considering multivitamins and adding protein shakes to my diet. My lack of energy had become a real problem.

It was only 8:00 p.m. or so when I entered the pool-house, which was, admittedly, a bit of a mess. Pots and pans were in the sink, clothes were strewn across the floor, and my bed was in a remarkable state of untidy-tude. However, despite the condition of my sheets, I managed to cover myself adequately.

I fell asleep in no time, even though Barrie was the last thing that caught my eye. He was sitting on top of a bookcase in my bedroom, staring at me, preparing himself for a long night of watching me sleep.

"There are two types of people in this world:
Those who are dumb enough to say and believe
there are only two types of people in the world,
and those who know there actually exists
somewhere between fifteen and twenty."

-DR. DRINKWATER

The House of Wayne

———◆———

A WEEK OR TWO LATER, I decided that I was long overdue for a formal visit with Wayne at the House of Wayne, also known as Spit House. I set off on foot and moseyed approximately two miles across the town of Needles to consult with the Patron-Saint-of-Hare-Brained-Schemes. I probably should have walked faster, though, as there was a chance that Wayne wouldn't be home. It was already 10:00 p.m. and I knew that he was supposed to report to his tollbooth by 11:00. The problem was it was such a pleasant night, I felt obligated to slow down and enjoy it. I guess I was willing to take the gamble.

My destination - The House of Wayne, also known as Spit House - is truly a marvel of architectural and landscape design. Although the structure is simply a brown, dreary, and poorly-maintained American Foursquare, it stands as a testament to the beauty of deterioration and decay. It also stands atop a hill and overlooks a beautiful vista of rumpled pavement, cracked cement, crumbling curbstones, and hundreds of improperly disposed of cigarette butts. The lawn begins at the front apron - a narrow wasteland completely devoid of grass - and is interrupted by the sidewalk. From there, the lawn continues onward approximately ten more yards until it reaches the front porch.

A concrete walkway filled with small fissures divides the front yard equally in half. Directly in the center of the left side is a sun-bleached Bathtub Mary, which rests amongst empty crumpled beer cans and discarded lottery tickets. On the right side, buried haphazardly in mud, is a decrepit, plastic, kiddie pool and a rusted mini-bike frame. The front of the house has only three windows, each with at least one broken pane of glass. In addition, the brown lead-based paint on the shingles has succumbed to age and weather. It's been chipping for years and accumulating like snowflakes around the foundation.

As the name of the house suggests, many locals enjoy driving to Spit House, stopping their cars, and spitting as far as they can onto the front yard. Some even claim to possess enough skill to spit as far as the welcome mat at the front door. It's a tradition, a special Town of Needles tradition, that even Wayne's family has grown to accept.

Six to One: Half a Dozen to the Other

———•———

I HASTENED MY SPEED WHEN I heard the sound of an ultra-pathetic skirmish - a donnybrook - taking place in my vicinity. I didn't run, but rather, walked briskly past the perfectly mani-cured front lawns and ubiquitous neighborhood rhododendrons of Needles. I was ninety-nine-point-nine-nine percent certain I knew the source of the barbaric screaming, heckling, and jeering. It's true, I thought of avoiding the whole scene, but curiosity, and a small amount of unrequited loyalty, pushed me onward. When I turned the corner, my prediction was confirmed.

On the front lawn of the House of Wayne, also known as Spit House, a disorderly disturbance - a riotous uproar of unparalleled stupidity - was in full steam.

Wayne was on the ground just beneath the gaze of Bathtub Mary, face first in the dirt - a recent victim of an inverted suplex. In order to inflict maximum pain upon Wayne, his brother, Serge, was on top of him, bending his arm back at an almost physically impossible angle. Wayne's pet capuchin monkey, the treacherous Choppinwood - named after his favorite composer - and his four elder brothers were lined up on the dilapidated front porch. They

were drunk with Molson Lights in hand, yelling out sinister con-
structive criticism to their beloved brother Serge.

"Pull his arm back moah!" Stefan said.

"Smothah his fahkin face in tha ground!" Yann added.

"Make that little bitch eat dirt!" Gervais interjected.

Fortunately, none of Wayne's quintuplet, French Canadian
brothers noticed me peering out at them from amidst their neighbor's rhododendrons. I was in a state of disbelief, beguiled even,
as I watched Wayne beaten to within an inch of his life. That's
when Serge leaned in closely to Wayne's ear and yelled at the top
of his lungs.

"You did it on purpose you fahkin shit-fah-brains! You fahkin
tanked the game!"

From the porch, Wayne's brother, Stefan, inserted an additional comment.

"Nevah-mind the game, that fahkin perv killed Mah!" he said.

Then, in perfect choral unison, Wayne's three remaining
brothers screamed:

"Nevah-mind Mah, he turned Dad into a fahkin' homo!"

"And yahr wearin' my wrinkle-free, pleated, stain-resistant
khakis, you scrahny-piece-of-shit!" said Serge, under his breath
in a slow, angry drawl.

After this last statement there was a lull in the action. Wayne
said nothing and remained perfectly still. It appeared as if he was
practicing some kind of passive, almost passing-out resistance —
his very own sick, masochistic form of civil disobedience.

But then, when it seemed as though the worst was nearly over
and Wayne's life would be spared, he defiantly uttered the following words.

"Serge, my dear brother," he said, "there's really no need to quarrel over sour strawberry milk. Not to mention, I believe you are mistaken about some par--tic--u--lar--ly important facts. These, yes these, are in fact, *MY* stain resistant, pleated, wrinkle-free, khaki pants – Dockers to be specific. I purchased them yesterday at Filene's Basement for five dollars and fifty-five cents – seventy-five-point-three percent off the original price of twenty-six dollars and ninety-nine cents."

Serge's face turned red with anger as he fell into an uncontrollable rage. He placed his hands around Wayne's throat and began to strangle and squeeze like a madman. In response, Wayne laughed and nonchalantly whimpered for air. Meanwhile, Choppinwood, Serge, and the rest of the quintuplets, clamored over who truly owned the cursed, stain-resistant pants.

At this precise moment, I realized I was witnessing a front yard fratricide right before my eyes. Against my better judgment, I revealed myself from within the rhododendrons, ran up behind Serge, and kicked the dumb bastard in the ass as hard as I possibly could. Serge released a guttural "ahhhhhh" and doubled over in pain.

Immediately after Serge's literal ass-kicking, the rest of the moronic quintuplet clan rushed on down from the porch upon me - like rabid hockey players finally released from a penalty box. One of them, most likely Stefan, directed the following syllables in my direction:

"Good thing yahr wearin' that fahkin homo-suit! Cuz this way the un-dah-take-ah ain't gonnah haf-tah waste time dressin' yah up fahr yah wake, bitch!"

Then he swung at me and connected with my left eye. I can't believe I gave him the opening.

Luckily, just after I was struck, the screen door of the House of Wayne, also known as Spit House, swung open and slammed against the front of the house. The quintuplets and Wayne's dads burst forth, outfitted in their navy-blue and black state police uniforms. Wayne's biological father, Gary, pumped the shotgun he carried. He aimed it skyward and shot off a load of pellets straight up at the moon.

"You fahkin-uncultured pussies!" he yelled.

"I thought yah fah-thaw and me told yahs!" added Nick, their non-biological father. "If yah gonna kill that god-forsaken Wayne, at least have the presents (he said presents not presence) of mind to do it in the back yahd for Christ's sake!"

"We've got to keep up appearances, yah know!" Gary retorted. "What'll tha fahkin neigh-bahs think of us now? Don't you know they already call this place Spit House! What's next? Shit House? They'll start getting out of their cahs and taken shits right in the front yahd?! Now, all of you, get the fahk off-ah my front lawn before I blow a fahkin shotgun load straight in-tah-yah ugly faces!"

With the barrel of a shotgun pointed at all of us, we promptly dispersed. It was quite clear that Gary and Nick meant business. After muttering threats on Wayne's life and making numerous unbecoming hand gestures, the quintuplets walked off down the street. They were headed in the direction of the Orchard Valley Tavern – a local bar filled to the brim with assholes. It isn't in, nor is it near, an orchard or valley of any kind.

CHAPTER 6 C

The Diaspora

———•———

AFTER WE WERE ORDERED OFF the front lawn of the House
of Wayne, also known as Spit-House, we made our way to the
garage to retrieve Wayne's wheels. His fine automobile - a rusty,
battered, baby-blue, Crown Victoria - was by its lonesome in the
two-car garage. For whatever reason, I guess just to test Wayne
and to humor myself, I elected to employ some simple reverse
psychology upon him.

"You know," I said, "I bet there isn't a single person in the
world who could completely turn your car around without leaving
the confines of this garage. It's not just humanly impossible, I'd
go so far as to say it's physically impossible. A matter of physics."

Wayne was disgusted by my supposed lack of faith and huffed
in mild annoyance.

"Each day," he replied, "each time the sun circles the Earth,
you become more and more of a nay-saying-n'er-do-well. Do you
know that, Barry? Are you conscious of your descent into pessi-
mism and misanthropy? You know what? Don't answer me. Just
try to look at the bright side once in a piggy-pink moon."

After those insulting-encouraging words, Wayne rushed to his car, settled into the driver's seat, and, without looking back, gave me the finger. He then began to lurch the Crown Victoria repeatedly backwards and forwards - an inch here, two centimeters there. And finally, twenty-five minutes later, Wayne successfully turned the Crown Victoria around one-hundred-and-eighty degrees. Of course, due to his maneuvering, the poor vehicle's bumpers acquired at least twice the number of pre-existing dings and scratches.

When he pulled out of the garage, he didn't say anything about his small, yet personally meaningful triumph. He simply drove the car up to me, opened the passenger side door, and said:

"Get in."

I asked Wayne where we were headed, but he neglected to answer the question. He pulled out of the driveway without checking for traffic and floored it down the street. And as his car shifted gears, so did his attitude. He suddenly seemed somewhat happy, randomly turned to me, and asked a suspicious question.

"So, what happened to your girlfriend?" he said.

I thought it was odd that he frequently asked about her, and I replied that I didn't know.

"I think she was cheating on you," he added.

"How would *you* know that?"

"It's generally known," he replied authoritatively.

Immediately after this less-than-detailed answer, I heard a loud thud, and realized the Crown Victoria was struck with what must have been a nearly full can of Molson Light. One of Wayne's quintuplet brothers had apparently made the difficult decision to sacrifice a bottle of his cherished beer. The need to add insult to Wayne's injuries must have overwhelmed him. The five of them started to yell at the car from the sidewalk in front of the Orchard Valley Tavern. Once again they reiterated what a "little bitch" they believed Wayne was. As luck would have it, they just happened to be on one of their cigarette breaks, and were delighted to have an another opportunity to terrorize their young brother.

Wayne ignored his brothers, took a sharp right turn way too fast, and darted down a side street.

There's no doubt he was a dangerous driver. On top of that, I'm certain nothing delighted him more than transporting trapped passengers in the seat next to him. For whatever reason, he genuinely enjoyed subjecting others to his suicidal driving and ill-advised vehicular exploits. He always claimed that he operated the Crown Victoria with the "utmost care" when others accompanied him, but the facts clearly suggest otherwise. Truth is, he loved to frighten the wits out of his passengers. In fact, several times after he performed one of his insane and reckless maneuvers, I swear I saw a faint smile - or at least a remnant of one - appear on his face.

Due to another ridiculous right turn, I hit the side of my head on the car window. Somehow, the collision with the glass jogged my memory. A millisecond after contact, I remembered that Wayne was a good forty-five minutes late for work.

I glanced over at him.

"I think you may be a little tardy for work," I said, and waited an uncomfortable amount of time for a reply. He appeared aloof, unconcerned, and irritated again.

"I'm bilocating right now," he eventually responded.

"You're what?"

"I'm at the tollbooth right now, but I'm also in the car with you. Do you understand?"

"No, not really. What is it that you're doing?"

He seemed even more agitated and provided a baffling clarification.

"Okay, fine," he said. "You're right. I'm not telling you the whole truth. I'm subletting my tollbooth to Philip."

"Your little brother mentee?"

"Yes, you heard me correctly."

I waited a moment and posed another question.

"So if you're not at the tollbooth," I asked, "where are you in addition to driving this car?"

"I'm sorry, but I can't tell you that."

"Why not?"

"I'm at an undisclosed location, okay? As you like to say 'it is what it is, c'est la vie.'"

"I never say either of those phrases."

"Listen, I refuse to provide the coordinates," he said in exasperation. "It's just not gonna happen. Not gonna happen."

"What about Philip then? Can you tell me about him?"

"Well, Barry, shit-for-brains, as you know I've adopted him as part of the Big Brothers Little Sisters program. He was a bit, as you often say, 'rough around the edges at first,' but he's come around quite nicely under my tutelage. I guess he's 'turned over a new leaf,' as you also like to say."

"He's at your tollbooth right now. Is that what you said?"

"Yes, dingleberries, that's what I said. It's my belief that working the night shift at a highway tollbooth is good experience for a twelve-year-old. It's that kind of real-world, rigorous, mentally-draining work that turns a boy into a man. His character strengthens car by car, minute by minute, ticket by ticket."

"Does he do anything else for you?" I inquired.

"Well, I would argue what he does for me, he does for himself. But if you must know, his last task was to roll two kegs into the woods for a high-school-bon-fire-party that I devised, but opted not to attend."

And then, just as I was about to ask Wayne why he organized a teenage keg party, he violently veered his car into a parking lot.

I guess it was time to complete task one of two.

"Wayne! You're not going to Annapolis.
You're going to the electric chair!"

-SISTER MARY

Thoughts communicated to Wayne concerning
his prospects of attending the United States
Naval Academy in Annapolis, Maryland

CHAPTER 7

The Accountant

———————

WE CAREENED INTO THE DENNY'S parking lot traveling at least forty-five-miles-an-hour. The Crown Victoria's tires screeched as it came to a remarkable halt, one inch from smashing into the breakfast mecca's brick wall. We landed next to a tan Volkswagen Beetle that looked to be decades-old and had a plant sticking out of its sunroof. While I examined the Bug, Wayne turned to me and stared dramatically and deeply into my eyes.

"Wait here," he said. "I have to meet briefly with my accountant."

I told him I thought a person needed money in order to have an accountant, but he ignored me, opened the car door, slammed the car door, and entered the restaurant.

Shortly after Wayne departed the vehicle, my eyes came upon his name, written in dust on the dash. I thought this observation was noteworthy. Even though writing his name in dust had always been a habit of his, he was definitely adding his signature to dirt more frequently.

Anyhow, after a grace period of sorts, I decided to investigate exactly what Wayne was up to in Denny's. I walked around the corner, stepped onto some bark mulch, and squeezed myself between some shrubbery. I then peered through a dirty side window and searched the brown, maroon, red, and yellow decor for the persons of interest. It didn't take long to spot Wayne and his accomplice. The place wasn't particularly busy, and the two of them were sitting at a booth in the corner, bathed in unflattering fluorescent light.

The man across from Wayne was bald and sported a curly mustache. A large white bib emanated from his collar and covered most of his chest. He was in the midst of eating a Grand Slam breakfast, which appeared to consist of pancakes, eggs, bacon, sausages, and plenty of syrup. A hapless waiter walked over to the table and delivered the bill. The accountant grabbed it, scrutinized it briefly, and handed it to Wayne. He then reached down into the booth next to him and produced a manila envelope. In mere seconds, Wayne passed some cash over the table and the manila envelope made its way in the opposite direction. Wayne then settled his debt with Denny's and walked obliquely to the front door. He looked confused.

Accordingly, I ran back to his car as fast as humanly possible. Oddly enough, though, Wayne didn't arrive for several more minutes. To pass the bonus in-between-time efficiently, I opened the glove compartment and found that it contained some thin-fingered gloves made of soft Italian leather. I reached in to try them on and a four by six card slipped out from under them. I quickly forgot the thrill of trying on silk-lined gloves and focused on the curious card. At the top of it, in blue ink and Wayne's chicken scratch, was the following heading:

"Goals For The Year."

Beneath that heading were typewritten objectives. Wayne must have used his Underwood Standard Portable Typewriter:

1. Sleep no longer than 10.5 hours on weekdays and 11 hours on weekends.
2. Do twenty-one push-ups, three days a week.
3. Start doing own laundry.
4. Submit inventions to companies.
5. Stop dumping paint cans, tvs, and major appliances in woods.
6. Don't be such a dick to Gary and Nick.
7. Consume daily-delicious medication.
8. Do sixteen push-ups twice a week, but never during weeks that contain religious holidays.

(Goal number two was crossed out and goal number eight was added in red ink).

CHAPTER 8

Asylum

———

EVENTUALLY, WAYNE RETURNED TO THE car and caught me with his index card in my hand. He inquired if I had "any respect for privacy," slapped my wrist, and jammed the card back into the glove compartment. He then asked me an idiotic, but memorable question.

"Do you know what $40,000 minus $700 is?" he said. "I've been standing in the front vestibule for the past couple of minutes and I can't seem to conjure up the answer."

"Are you kidding me?" I responded angrily, while looking at my freshly struck arm.

"I most certainly am not."

"Why didn't you run that one by your accountant, Wayne?"

"Are you going to answer or not?" he said. "I don't want to rub Peter to piss off Paul, if you know what I mean."

"No, I don't know what you mean. No one knows what you mean."

"Just answer the question," he demanded. "I don't exactly have all the time in the world."

"$39,300, Wayne. $39,300."

The second I said $39,300 for the second time, Wayne turned the key in the ignition and blindly backed out of his parking space.

For reasons that are unclear to me, he was in a tremendous rush, and, subsequently, blew through a stop sign. He was then forced into an extreme, death-defying-peel-out to avoid the row of cars barreling down upon us. I suggested that perhaps it would be a good idea to slow down a wee-bit, but I was quickly rebuffed. Wayne assured me that he was driving "quite safely" and had "everything totally under control." He was utterly aghast at the mere notion that he was driving to endanger, so I chose to lay off the subject altogether.

We traveled in the Crown Victoria in total silence for a particularly long time. I wanted to ask Wayne where we were headed, but thought better of it. He rarely announced his destination prior to arrival - as was his custom. After a while, though, Wayne piped up and broke the silence.

"Why are you wearing that suit?" he inquired. "Are you mourning something?"

I answered, but I could tell he wasn't listening. Instead, he swerved off the road and drove up to a security trailer at the abandoned Needles State Psychiatric Hospital. He asked me to crouch down as low as possible, got out of the car, and knocked on the trailer door three times. An old man in a blue security uniform emerged and began to talk with him. I watched carefully as Wayne placed something or other into the old man's hands. He then returned to the car and drove by the trailer. Soon enough, we found ourselves approaching the heart of the hospital.

The two of us pulled up to the brick building that used to house the patients of Needles State. The building's nine wings still exist, along with a once wonderful, now crumbling, decrepit courtyard. All of the windows and doors were boarded up with red-painted plywood. All windows and doors except for, of course, the door Wayne discovered – a forgotten entrance, hidden behind some out-of-control rhododendrons.

I followed Wayne, who was armed with a flashlight, and the two of us disappeared behind the door. We walked through hallway after hallway, past chipped paint and water damage, immature graffiti and mutilated filing cabinets. In one room, which must have been a break room, there were still half-sludge-filled coffee cups resting on a table. They looked as if they had been sitting there since the place shut down ten or twenty years ago.

Ultimately, Wayne and I found ourselves standing in the courtyard. It was a beautiful, clear night and neither of us said a word for a minute or two. I looked up at the sky. A cool wind hit my face and prompted me to consider how peaceful and calming the hospital became when its doors were closed. Since its been shuttered, it's probably twice as effective at soothing nerves than it ever had been. I understand why Wayne sought solace at a place that most would do anything to avoid.

Then Wayne turned to me and looked me in the eyes.

"I come here a lot," he said. "Mr. Markoff found out I'm addicted to this place. Now he charges me an admission fee. I know that makes him sound like an asshole, but he's actually a good guy. Just goes to show you how a person shouldn't judge a cover by the book."

"How long have you been haunting this courtyard?" I asked.

He replied after a minute or two - sans eye contact.

"I didn't kill my mother," he said solemnly.

"I know, Wayne."

"My mother died when she gave birth to me. Post-partum-hemorrhaging. Extreme loss of blood. I didn't do it," Wayne explained.

"I know. I'm sorry."

"Then again, maybe I did kill her," he continued, while staring at the ground. "I mean, she had quintuplets before me and there were no problems at all. They say she complained of no pain what-so-ever during their births. My brothers told me she enjoyed every minute she was in labor with them."

"Well, it's all terribly ironic. There's no doubt about that."

"They remind me of it almost daily," he declared and looked skyward, forlornly. "They say I'm a natural born killer. I entered the world with sin...But I guess that's how the cookie crumbles, as you like to say."

"I don't think I've ever said that."

"I suppose I also played a part in my father going gay. You know?"

"I'm pretty sure he already was gay."

"Well," he said, "if my mother hadn't died, he never would have married Nick. I know that for a fact. I thought they were just partners at work. I never thought they'd become partners in life."

"I guess that's just how the cookie crumbles sometimes," I said. "State police detectives have to work closely with one another."

"Now, they're partners on and off duty," Wayne mumbled.

"Look at the bright side: They must save a considerable amount of money on gas, car-pooling to work every day."

"Yeah, that's definitely true," Wayne noted. "I never looked at it that way."

He paused, collected his thoughts, and continued.

"At least my mother's death reminded my father about the precariousness of life. At least he's living honestly, freely, and on his own terms."

"That can't be denied," I agreed.

Then, somewhat randomly and after a brief delay, Wayne brought up the subject of his pants.

"These are my pants, Barry," he said. "They are *my* pants. *My* khaki-pleated-wrinkle-free-stain-resistant-pants. Sure, I did borrow Serge's khaki pants, but I lost them...and those pants were only pleated and wrinkle-free, not stain-resistant. These pants are mine. I bought them to replace the ones I lost. Serge is mistaken, greatly mistaken. I have been wronged."

"My husband wanted Gerry to be named Darvon, but I said 'No, absolutely not.' I told him Gerry would be named Gerry and our next child would be named Darvon. Fortunately, we neglected to have another human child. Instead, we adopted a fur child and named him Darvon. Of course, I wanted him to be named Foibles, but so much for that."

-PRISCILLA DRINKWATER

The Basketball Game, According to Wayne

———

OBVIOUSLY, ACCORDING TO THE MIND of Wayne, the debacle overseen by Bathtub Mary and the rest of us was not just about pants - it was also about principle. It didn't matter that his logic was flawed. It was all quite reasonable to him: They were his pants, and, therefore, he would rather die than relinquish them. Often, though, bigger issues manifest themselves through smaller ones. Clearly, the events that transpired earlier that day at the basketball game were on his mind. And it was in the courtyard, under the stars, in the middle of a former insane asylum, that Wayne finally made sense and delivered the following, unsolic-ited, monologue. I'm pretty sure he just wanted to hear himself talk.

"See, my brothers formed an intramural basketball team a couple months back," he said. "The five of them make up the whole team, no substitutes. They call themselves The Bomberos, the Spanish term for a legendary Mexican monster that's one-half man, one-fourth bull, and the rest marmot. The Bomberos play against local teenagers – middle school students and some high school kids – who were cut from the Needles High basketball team.

"Anyhow, as one would probably guess, my brothers, being French-Canadian, are terrible basketball players. It's just not in their blood. Still, they have two distinct advantages. First, they are quintuplets and are, therefore, awfully confusing to defend. Second, they're older and significantly bigger and stronger when compared to their sometimes pre-pubescent competitors.

"Due to these advantages, The Bomberos have compiled an amazing record. They've won all of their games – not with talent or finesse – but with muscle and kamikaze play. However, one contingent attempted to block The Bombero's path to an undefeated season: parents. The parents who attend the games started to complain. In response, league organizers came up with a plan to appease these parents and, at the same time, soften the blow to the Bomberos. The plan was this: Instead of taking direct action and banning The Bomberos altogether, they made it a requirement that all teams must have at least six players. Naturally, parents were upset with this decision. They anticipated The Bomberos would've been banned outright. But alas, the powers that be thought that would be too dangerous. It's my belief the officials must have feared they would be accused of French-Canadian basketball discrimination.

"Most would think this rule would benefit The Bomberos. Toward the finales of many of their games, at least one of my brothers would foul out and they'd have to play short-handed. But they were angered, greatly angered – like a bear with sore balls. As predicted, they even considered quitting the league. The thought of adding another team member, joining forces with a second-rate-foreigner - extending their coalition - was inconceivable to them.

And that's when an idea dawned upon Stefan.

"Stefan approached me this morning and told me about the predicament he and my brothers were facing. He started sweet-talking me, saying how much the team needed my help, how sorry he and my brothers were for mistreating me all these years. He told me how beautiful I looked in the outfit I was wearing. He even said there was something magical about the way the sunlight streamed through the window and played upon my face.

"Then, he asked me if I was willing to be the Bomberos' sixth player, a much coveted position that has never been offered to anyone other than myself. He said I probably wouldn't get any playing time, but he still wanted me to be there with them. You know, show my support from the bench.

"Finally, it seemed as though my brothers needed me for something. I couldn't resist his offer. I accepted the sixth-player-bench-position without a second thought."

Wayne Tanks the Game

———◆———

"This evening's game," Wayne continued, "was an *important* one for my brothers, and all the best people - the right people - were there. The Bomberos were matched up against the Yiff-Yiffs, whose tallest and oldest member is Lloyd Wilkins, a tenacious five-foot-seven-thirteen-year-old. Since The Bomberos had yet to face the Yiffs, the winner of the contest would stand alone as the first place team in the league.

"When the ball was thrown into the air for the opening tip off, fans in the stands had no idea they were about to witness a series of events that would not be easily forgotten. The tension in the gymnasium was palpable. Per usual, my brothers struck with a vengeance, with an overwhelming force no team could ever be expected to withstand. The Bomberos kept their pimpled enemies off balance and penetrated their defenses time after time. Despite their poor accuracy, they dropped so many bombs that just enough were on target to establish a significant lead. Going into the fourth quarter, they were up by fifteen.

"However, midway through the fourth quarter, it was clear The Bomberos had overextended themselves. Their offensive play could no longer be sustained. They just plain ran out of gas. And as their lead dwindled, my brothers became increasingly frustrated. They were desperate and started to foul left and right.

"That's when the unexpected happened: Gervais was actually blocked by one of the Yiffs. His shot was knocked off its trajectory, hit his head, bounced off, and landed in the stands – the ultimate humiliation in the game of basketball. Gervais was thirsty for revenge. So, on the very next play, he acted as if he was going for the ball and clothes-lined Lloyd Wilkins. Gervais' ruse didn't fool the referee. A technical foul was called and Gervais protested. He told the ref he was going to stick his foot up his ass, and was promptly ejected from the game.

"That's when I entered the contest. I took my place at the key, and watched Lloyd as he easily drained both of his foul shots. At that point, The Yiff-Yiffs were down by two, but with ten seconds left, still had possession of the ball. They did some kind of confusing, elaborate set play that only tweens could come up with, and the ball was passed to their star Lloyd. Lloyd, from a particularly far distance from the basket, tossed up a risky Hail-Mary three pointer. It swished through the net.

"And what do you know? All of a sudden, I found myself standing by my lonesome, two-thirds of the way down the court. For some reason, I really don't know why, Jean whipped the ball directly at me. I caught it, and dribbled to the basket as the final seconds of the game ticked away. That's when I attempted an awkward, half-assed lay-up, similar to what Edwardian gentleman would do. I missed. I missed badly. The buzzer buzzed and the ball clanked on the underside of the rim. I thought the game was over. But, to my dismay, I discovered that I had been *fouled*.

"So there I was – standing alone at the line at the top of the key for what seemed like an eternity. The entire gymnasium fell perfectly quiet – everyone, everything – blurred all around me. I'm fairly certain, for that brief moment, the world almost stopped and went into slow motion. For the first time in a long time, I was in the zone. I could think absolutely clearly.

"My four remaining brothers stood at the key underneath the rim. They stared intently at me with a look that said, 'If you don't hit at least one of these shots, we're going to have you drawn and quartered, you treacherous bastard.' I think they could tell by my pathetic, Edwardian-dandy-lay-up attempt that my heart just wasn't in it.

"But this was my chance to be a noble warrior, to help topple their regime. Yeah, it's true, those small kids on the Yiff-Yiffs will probably become just like my quintuplet brothers when they get older. But hey, maybe not – who knows?

"Anyhow, I decided to actually aim for the basket. I knew that way I would be destined to miss. True to form, I did – my first shot ricocheted against the backboard. Didn't even touch the rim.

"I only had to miss one more time. The referee returned the ball to me. I took it, bounced it three times, aimed, and let fate take over for me. Unfortunately, this foul shot was a hell-of-a-lot closer. The ball did one of those things where it rolls around the rim a million times. My heart sank every time it looked as if it would fall through the net. But then, thankfully, the ball rolled off the rim and landed in Lloyd's outstretched hands.

Game over.

"The crowd went berserk. Luckily, due to all of the commotion, I was able to absquatulate through an emergency exit. I ran - chugged - as fast as I could all the way home. I knew I had to get my things and disappear before my brothers arrived."

"Yes, that's true. And I was in two bands, as a matter of fact. The first one I created was known as Perry Wynkle and the Non-Sequiturs. Unfortunately, people often mispronounced Wynkle - the W and the Y should sound like a V. Anyway, we released two albums: *Plaid on Plaid Crime* followed by *Contributing to the Delinquency of Miners.*

My next band was known as Dewey Decimal and the Parenthetical Citations. Our one and only album was titled *Unintentional Infliction of Emotional Distress.*

Sadly, both bands broke up due to *Irreconcilable Differences*, which, as you might guess, is the title of my solo album.

-WAYNE

CHAPTER 10

The Awakening

———————

WAYNE FINALLY FINISHED SPEAKING AND turned to me as if he actually wanted to hear my reaction. I didn't want to let him down, so I came up with some words to fill the air.

"Yeah," I said, "believe it or not, what you did was a good, quasi-quisling, kind of thing to do. You helped those meek little shits to prevail. I guess."

His face molded itself into this quizzical, dumbfounded look I don't think I've ever seen a human face form. He squinted his right eye and his left brow descended a little bit. His right cheek pushed upwards toward his forehead and his nose shriveled. And somehow, while he maintained this unique expression on his face, he requested clarification.

"What? What do you mean, the meek?" he asked.

It was a strange moment. For the first time in a long time Wayne decided to listen to me. So, I explained to him that he sort of acted like a martyr – except, of course, he didn't die, or at least, his brothers hadn't killed him yet. I then told him about the meek inheriting the Earth, a concept he had never encountered before in his life. And, all of a sudden, he seemed really proud of himself. I guess I managed to replace a faulty fuse in his brain. I could tell that a light bulb had come to life and started to shine in the empty attic of his head.

About a half an hour later that night, Wayne dropped me off at the pool-house. Before I got out of the car, I noticed a sad, contemplative expression materialize on his face. While he stared at his name in the dust on the dash, he proceeded to tell me how humans "live in a dog eat dog world" and that we're "all by ourselves."

"We're born alone, and we die alone," he declared.

I don't think he meant a word of it – and I told him so. I'm pretty sure he was just in a momentary mood and he wanted to appear philosophical and profound. In fact, he was probably parroting someone else who said those words – a person who wanted to rationalize the crooked-screw-job he or she had just given someone else.

Anyhow, I said goodbye and disappeared into the darkness on the way back to the pool-house. It's funny - at the time I hadn't the faintest idea how my seemingly innocuous comments about the meek would affect Wayne.

CHAPTER 11

The Moonlight, The Pool, and Gary-Spelled-Like-Gerry

———

I ALMOST MISSED THE RED envelope taped to the gate. Sure, it was right in front of me, but I wasn't quite in tune with the present. Instead, I was thinking about the evening I spent with Wayne as I fiddled with the combination lock and robotically aligned the numbers. When they were in proper order, I pulled down, gained entry, and gazed straight toward the pool. And that's when I saw it there. My name was in the middle of it, capitalized in big bold letters - **BARRY**.

I closed the gate behind me and immediately felt the presence of the pool. Although it was hidden beneath a cloak of darkness, I could hear the pump buzzing and the heater humming, the water lapping and gently brushing against the walls. I pictured what it would look like with the lights on and made that image a reality. I squeezed myself between the fence and some bushes and flipped the switch. Then, I made my way to the shallow-end stairs and looked out upon the blue water. It was crystal clear, illuminated by a bright white light under the diving board.

I stood there for maybe ten seconds or so until my moment of reflection was interrupted. A voice emanated from a foot or two behind-below and startled me.

"What's that in your hand, Barry?" it asked. "Can I see it?"

I recognized my meddlesome inquisitor's small voice before I even laid eyes upon him.

It was Gary-Spelled-Like-Gerry.

The little bastard was standing in my blind spot, as he so often does.

I turned to face him.

"Pardon me?" I muttered angrily - even though I heard him perfectly well.

Gary-Spelled-Like-Gerry could tell I was annoyed and compensated by reverting to his wide-eyed and bashful routine. He gripped his hands behind his back and looked toward his feet. He then pointed his left foot downward and skimmed it - side to side - over the cement several times.

"I was just wah-wah-wondering what that red awn-vah-lope is da-da-doing in your hand," he stammered. "Could I ba-ba-borrow it for a second?"

I answered him with a stare and without saying a word. He knew I was displeased with his query, so he kept his eyes fixed to the ground. He did the best he could to avoid matching my glare. I considered waiting him out - thinking he would retreat if I didn't answer. Within seconds, however, I decided I wanted to be free of his bull-shit as soon as possible.

Thus, I answered his foolish questions with further questions.

"Why do you have to stick your nose in my shit, Gary-Spelled-Like-Gerry?" I asked hostilely. "Besides, I haven't even opened the envelope yet. Why the fuck do you need to read it before me?"

His pupils moved to the top of his eye sockets. He pretended to be interested in the nighttime sky.

"I ja-ja-just thought I…"

I stopped him right there and re-directed.

"It's not going to happen, Gary-Spelled-Like-Gerry. Not going to happen. Now, tell me what you really want so you can be on your way."

Gary-Spelled-Like-Gerry appeared confused and took a moment to collect his rather simple thoughts.

Despite some initial difficulty, he managed to speak up again.

"Da-da-do you think life," he said, "must have been really ba-ba-boring for people in the past?"

"That's what's on your mind right now, huh?"

"Yes."

"No, it wasn't boring."

"Well, wah-wah-why not?"

"I don't know for sure, Gary-Spelled-Like-Gerry, but I think people didn't have time to be bored. Most probably lived day to day and did whatever they could to survive."

He wasn't satisfied with my answer and continued his absurd argument.

"Yeah, bah-bah-but still, everything was in black and wah-wah-white."

"What?"

"Everything was in bah-bah-black and wah-wah-white," he affirmed.

"Okay, I heard you - despite your pseudo stuttering act. Now you need to explain yourself."

My request for clarification further upset Gary-Spelled-Like-Gerry. His voice became thinner and creaked more than usual. He sounded like he was running out of oxygen.

On the defensive and the verge of tears, he made his case.

"In history class, Ba-Ba-Barry," he explained. "Sometimes in history cah-cah-class, we watch these videos about the pa-pa-past. They're in bah-bah-black and wah-wah-white. Just like old movies and tah-tah-television from a long time ago. So-so-so, that must have been before cah-cah-color was added to the world. It must have been bah-bah-boring without-out color."

Gary-Spelled-Like-Gerry took two steps back and his body appeared to shrink in size by twenty-percent. He then looked me in the eyes, cautiously-pleadingly, knowing full-well what type of reaction was in store for him.

Accordingly, we entered into another silent duel. Neither of us moved or said a word. We simply looked into one another's eyes and considered the possibilities for the immediate future. I spent the time concocting a plan to capture Gary-Spelled-Like-Gerry and throw him into the pool - condition him with a positive punishment. He, however, was busy contemplating the fastest escape route available to him. Strangely enough, though, I could also tell he felt torn: He actually maintained a sliver of hope I would consider his asinine statements. It must have been difficult for him to entertain two thoughts at once.

Eventually, I broke off the staring stalemate and looked down and to my right. I tried to be subtle about it, but Gary-Spelled-Like-Gerry perceived my change in focus almost instantaneously.

That's when I realized it was do or die. I lunged for my weapon: a pool leaf skimmer, attached to a ten-foot aluminum pole. Alas, Gary-Spelled-Like-Gerry - simultaneously - made a bold move: He ran directly past me, his feet nimbly negotiating the border of the pool and concrete. No doubt about it, experience and learning from his mistakes turned him into a formidable escape artist. He read my thoughts properly. The diminutive dolt knew he needed the pool to be between himself and the reach of my net and metal beam.

Next thing I knew, the two of us had reached yet another temporary, but significant impasse: We were both equidistant from the gate. At this point, though, I was sick of our cat and mouse game. Therefore, I feigned genuine pursuit for a few yards, stopped short, and watched as Gary-Spelled-Like-Gerry completed his vanishing act. All I saw was a blur of a brother as he jumped over a corner of the pool and whisked through the exit. I suppose someone must have hit a fast-forward button for him.

I've never seen another human being travel so swiftly and efficiently.

But, more importantly, I finally had the pool to myself.

Sans Gary-Spelled-Like-Gerry, my first course of action was to prepare the HMS Talbot for embarkment. Thing is, I knew it would be best to read the contents of the red envelope while floating in my reliable yellow vessel. I've found that news, especially bad news, should be read while buoyant and in a state of repose. Hence, I used the skimmer to drag the boat to the stairs, cleared some pine needles from it, and carefully climbed aboard. Not a single drop of water landed on my suit.

It took longer than usual to satisfactorily adjust myself in the Talbot, but, after some delicate movements, I finally managed to find the perfect position. I rested my head on the bow and my feet, which were crossed, dangled over the stern, just above the water. At last - in fitting formation - I tore open the envelope and discarded its remnants here and there on deck. I then held the letter about a foot above my face and began reading.

It said the following:

INVITATION TO BRUNCH

Dearest Barry,

I request the honour of your presence for brunch this Sunday, the twentieth of September, at precisely twelve o'clock.

Traditional breakfast and lunch dishes will be offered. They may or may not include:

Buttermilk beignets with salted maple-caramel sauce (for dipping)

Smoked salmon and avocado tartare with Williams' Bon Chrétien pear

Quiche Lorraine with seasonal greens and crumbled Bulgarian feta

Parfait with steel cut oats, Greek yogurt, dried cranberries, apricots, and kiwi

Sparkling or still mineral water and an assortment of teas will also be available.

Please do not bring any guests.

Wayne is most definitely **not** invited.

No need to RSVP. I know you will be in attendance.

Your mother,
Priscilla Drinkwater

P.S. Dress code = Formal elegance. Suit and tie required.
No tennis shoes.
P.P.S. Tradition is synonymous with respect.

"As soon as I open my mouth, I'm no longer myself."

-BARRY DRINKWATER

CHAPTER 12

Two of Three

———◆———

I STAND AT ONE END of a massive, dimly lit, marble room. It's empty, except for what looks like a fountain, fifty feet in front of me. The oblong chamber has no exit in sight - I think it must be some kind of mausoleum. As that thought resonates, a wave of paranoia sweeps over my body. I turn to see what's behind me. A gigantic door is there, between two Corinthian columns, under an elegantly carved entablature. I grab the knob and try to twist, but it won't move. Locked. I swivel once more and survey my surroundings.

The room I'm in is thirty or forty feet wide and at least a hundred feet long. The vaulted ceiling rises a good fifty feet over my head. I touch the wall next to me. My hand presses against the cold, smooth, and solid marble. My mind registers - for the first time - something I should have recognized earlier: the sound of raindrops, hundreds of them, falling and splashing into pools of water. I zero in at the fountain ahead of me. It's enormous, obscured by a patchy fog.

Next thing I know, I'm standing in heavy mist at the foot of the fountain. I feel dwarfed by its size as I look up, my head tilted at sixty-five degrees. It's difficult to see in its entirety, but I can tell it has two circular levels, the middle wider than the top, and a reservoir base. On the top level are the remains of two legs - wholly devoid of a body above them - one from the lower thigh to the foot, the other from the knee to the foot. On the tier in the middle, I see scattered pieces of a body - an arm here, a hand there, and parts of a crumbled torso. At the base, in the pool in front of me, I see what's left of the statue - most notably a marble head on its side, an Archaic smile faintly visible on its face.

As I inspect the fountain, the drips plunge from tier to tier, one after another, and lull me into a sleepy state. I'm groggy and I don't register the murmurs that softly hum and reverber-ate throughout the room. But then I come to and shake off my temporary trance. I crane my neck to look beyond the fountain, and figures appear, partially shrouded by fog. I don't know how long I was standing there, unaware of their presence. I walk closer and discover two men, an older man and a younger one, standing before me. The two are side-by-side, examining an oil painting of a fox-hunt in progress. I wonder where the painting came from, and notice that it's not alone. There are other pieces, in large, heavy gilded frames, that surround it on the wall.

The two men complete their analysis and walk away - knowingly and without a word - toward the far side of the mau-soleum. About ten feet in front of me, they abruptly, but slowly, stop in their tracks and turn to face me. The two look upon me with hollow stares, and the father says something to me in gib-berish, which, somehow, I can understand. They want me to fol-low them. I consent and cautiously pursue until they disappear through a nearby doorway. I approach and find that the gateway is narrow and difficult to navigate. Still, I manage to squeeze my way through and enter an adjoining room.

The room is made of white marble, dimly-ghoulishly lit, and empty. The two men are standing directly in the middle of it and appear irritable, as if they've been waiting too long. The second they see me, the younger man says something to the older one, coldly, in gibberish. This time, I can't understand a word. The older man nods his head, and the two immediately leave the room.

After a moment or two, I follow suit and attempt to exit the way I entered. The doorway, however, has morphed into a passageway. I lift myself into it and begin to crawl my way back to the fountain room. I wriggle and worm and feel as if I'm moving upward in a large block of Swiss cheese. Eventually, my foot gets stuck. Then my arm. Then my torso. I reach the point where I can only move my head. And that's when I realize I'm trapped - like a prehistoric mosquito in solidified amber. Just before I panic, I tune into the muted sound of water dripping in the distance. The droplets fall, from one pool to another, non-stop.

"There's a place for people who laugh at nothing."

-SISTER MARY

Her words while punishing Wayne and pointing –
north by northwest - toward Needles Mental Hospital

Small Sacrifices

———◆———

THE FOLLOWING IS AN EXAMPLE of my mother's column that's featured weekly in the Needles News Tribune. It's a sensational story and raises more questions than answers. Let's just say I'm skeptical of the details.

The Slasher Hiding in the Basement
by Priscilla Drinkwater

Little did thirty-three-year-old parents, Miranda and Burt Higglebottom, know their laundry trip to the basement would end in torture and murder. The elementary school music teacher and her family had just returned home from StoryLand (Glen, New Hampshire at the junction of Route Sixteen and Route Thirty-two) after a day full of joy and golden memories - memories that should have lasted a lifetime. Instead, their day - and their lives - ended with shrieks of terror and deep pools of blood. Yes, little did poor Miranda and Burt know they were to launder their clothes for the last time in their lives. They had no idea that Dante Gonzago, a thirty-five-year-old, under-employed, former line cook, was awkwardly hiding between the furnace and the boiler. He was there, waiting to slash their faces and bodies with an extremely rare, fifteenth century samurai sword.

In the early evening hours of August tenth, Dante Gonzago allegedly broke into the basement of the Higglebottom house by way of a partially open bulkhead. It was there, as previously noted, that Gonzago, painfully cramped between the furnace and the boiler, jumped out at the husband and wife. "I don't want your valuables," he screamed. "I just want your lives." Instantly, the bloodbath began, which resulted in the deaths of a dutiful mother, her doting, engineer husband, and their three young sons: little Tad, quick-witted Quentin, and the oh-so-curious Webster. The Higglebottoms' neighbor, Randy Sid Winkiewicz, must have been absolutely horrified when he stumbled upon the dismembered torsos, heads, arms, legs, hands, feet, fingers, and toes scattered throughout the house.

Only a half hour prior to the murders, Randy Sid was at home watching a television show about history's most notorious serial killers. At the conclusion of the program, he went out for a walk and bought some scratch tickets. When he returned, he noticed his neighbor's open bulkhead and a trail of blood that led to the cellar. Brave Randy Sid traveled down the stairs and discovered that the Higglebottoms had been sliced into a million pieces - and will never be put together again.

Later that night, Dante Gonzago was apprehended for his horrendous deeds. He has since pleaded not guilty and insists on his innocence. Prosecutors say they will pursue the death penalty, as the murders occurred in New Hampshire.

This story perfectly exemplifies the dreadful facts: Sixty percent of homicides are committed for no reason and can happen at any time, killers who use samurai swords are seventy percent more likely to dismember their victims' bodies than normal-every-day murderers, and finally, homes in the United States are broken into, on average, seventeen hundred times every thirty-three seconds.

Dr. Orval Billingtons, Psychiatrist-in-Chief at Needles General Hospital, a scholar who possesses a litany of higher learning degrees (M.D., DMD, DPM, VMD, Psy.D, Ph.D), had this to say about killers like Mr. Gonzago:

"I know exactly how the mind of a killer like Dante's works. I know the dark secrets he's hiding. I know what he's thinking… I know all-too-well, in fact. Killers like him are out there among us and some are very, very clever. They're cagey, difficult to find. They're resourceful and often use aliases – a sign of an individual who possesses true anti-social tendencies."

This story just goes to show that people can kill you and your family whether they have a reason to or not. Take Dante Gonzago for instance: Friends and neighbors describe him as "pretty normal" and "outgoing, some of the time." His best friend, Lenny Wilberforce, was recently interviewed about the murder.

"Maybe," Mr. Wilberforce said, "Dante might attempt to steal a purse from an old, frail woman or burglarize a Mom and Pop type store. But, I have to say, I'd never guess he'd cut a young couple and their three children to pieces. And, you know, I've always had a couple of questions: Why would he do it for no reason at all? How could he afford a fifteenth century samurai sword?"

Well, I guess we'll never know the answers to those questions. Let us all pray that Dante gets what he deserves: a speedy and fair death by lethal injection. Please check out the following Stop Home Invaders Safety Tips. They might just save your life.

Safety Tips
Five Simple Ways To Protect Yourself From Home Invaders

1. An Electric Fence – Adding an electric fence to the perimeter of your home is a real no-brainer. Not only will the fence prove to criminals you're probably crazier than they are, but you can kill two birds with one stone and keep sheep and other farm animals on your property. This way, you'll have fewer reasons to leave the house and risk your life in the outside world. You'll also have the opportunity to make your clothing from scratch and produce your own dairy products. You may even qualify for small farm tax breaks!

2. Identification Monitors and a Mail-Box Rope and Pulley System – Mailmen, U.S. Census Bureau workers, tax appraisers, door-to-door salesmen, Jehovah's Witnesses, and Gypsies who want to coat your driveway, are all behind a large percentage of home intrusions. Be careful: Home invaders often pose as one of the above transgressors. How can you avoid these characters all together? Build a rope and pulley system or use pneumatic tubes to get your mail. You should also install identification monitors - complete with retinal and hand print scanning

apparatus. You can never be too sure who steps foot onto your property, and, ultimately, into your life.

3. A Shotgun – You should store a loaded shotgun in the closet next to your bed. Guns save lives. They save lives by taking lives. Just imagine how you'll feel when you finally get the opportunity to blow an intruder away. There's nothing more thrilling than running to the safe room after a righteous kill.

4. Neighbors – Don't trust them. Don't talk to them. Definitely don't tell them your work schedule or when you will be on vacation. Neighbors only want to do two things:
   A. Break into your house
   B. Spy on you while you're changing in and out of your pajamas

   There is a reason for the saying "The grass is always greener on the other side." Your neighbors are envious of you and they want to see you naked, destroyed, or both.

5. The Bulkhead – Try to close the bulkhead properly. When a bulkhead is fastened correctly, the chances of someone breaking into your basement decrease by at least fifty percent. That number comes from a recent study released by People for Safe and Secure Basements, a non-profit think tank based in Washington, D.C.

"Eventually, I'll be so filthy rich that I'll do nothing but walk around my back yard in a beautiful, long flowing robe. I'll wander aimlessly to and fro, without a care in the world. I'll tend to the rhododendrons, the gardenias, the peonies, back to the rhododendrons - any sort of flower or shrubbery that temporarily suits my fancy. Every now and then, however, I'll pause to let pigeons eat peanuts from the palms of my hands. They'll have absolute trust in me and approach single file - one by one - patiently and discreetly. Should you happen to appear in my yard, I may even toss a couple of peanuts toward your feet. Why, you ask? Well, because it's inevitable that I'll pity you in the future. But don't worry: I won't look down at you. No, I'll avoid eye contact with you at all costs. I won't be able to bear the sight of you nibbling on those peanuts. Yes, you, nibbling like a frantic, flustered, fidgety squirrel."

-WAYNE

Comments conveyed to Barry shortly before Wayne's awakening and accompanying transformation

Prelude to a Brunch

———◆———

LIFE WAS UNEVENTFUL FOR ABOUT two weeks after receipt of the brunch invitation. I went about my regular routine - kept the pool in tip-top shape - and didn't see much of anyone. Things changed, though, on the morning of Sunday, September the twentieth.

I woke up around quarter to twelve and I could sense that something didn't seem quite right. I had this feeling, a feeling that someone - an extreme asshole, to be specific - was in my vicinity. Of course, I thought the idea of sensing someone in my bones was nonsensical, but my instincts turned out to be correct. Within a minute, I recognized the sound of footsteps making their way along the white pebble path. Next, I heard keys jingle-jangling, followed by the manhandling of a doorknob. Someone meant business.

Naturally, I was fully prepared for imminent attack when the trespassing moron managed to open the door. My survival skills are first-rate, so they kicked in immediately upon hearing the pool-home invasion in progress: I crawled out of bed, rubbed my eyes, grabbed the wiffle ball bat under my nightstand, and quietly sauntered across the bedroom. I then concealed myself between the wall and my armoire, ready to fight for my property and self-respect.

I quickly deduced the unlawful intruder was a novice who felt uncomfortable - possibly guilty - about impinging on my privacy. The interloper attempted to be quiet while walking through my dwelling, but stumbled several times, and even knocked what sounded like a fully built Jenga tower onto the floor. Needless to say, it was easy to trace his or her movements through the living room and the kitchen.

After a minute or so, the pool-house-burglar was standing at the entrance to my quarters. The door slowly opened and the sunlight spread - from an acute to an obtuse angle - throughout my room. Soon, the door was completely open and a squirrelly, academic-looking man cautiously entered. When I first saw him - with his back to me - he appeared to be nibbling at something. His head was pointed downward and his hands shifted nervously back and forth at his mouth - like a typeball moving across a sheet of paper.

I kept my location a secret and watched the fussy scoundrel as he made his way around my room. Due to my position, I never saw his face - only his posterior and occasionally a side view of his body. Still, I monitored his movements carefully and watched him pick up my belongings, inspect them briefly, and set them down in slightly different positions. He even picked up Barrie and did something or other to his head. Before long, though, he opted to sit himself down on my bed, next to the nightstand.

I can't say I was pleased that a stranger perched himself on my bed, but I was reluctant to disrupt the natural flow of pure aberrant behavior. True, I wanted the guy out of my room, but I was curious to see just what the sordid bastard would do next - and he didn't disappoint me. In a move that's almost too horrifying to be true, he swiveled his body toward the headboard and began to closely examine my pillow. I couldn't tell what he was doing at first, but eventually I put two and two together: He was searching for strands of my hair. I saw him pick up several, using his pointer finger and thumb, and delicately place them in a plastic sandwich bag. Then, he folded the bag a few times and deposited it in his suitcoat pocket.

After he stuffed my hair in his pocket, my perpetrator took a moment to longingly eye my pillow. Initially, it appeared that he was searching for yet another follicle, but he had other plans. Abruptly, he stooped downward and surprisingly, but not so surprisingly, burrowed his head into my pillow. When he got his fill of that maneuver, he raised his head slightly and gingerly sniffed the cushion, treating it as if it were a fine wine. He even moved his nose around the surface of it in a circular motion - counterclockwise. Finally, he placed his face at the center of the pillow and deeply inhaled its essence into his lungs.

The inhalation sound was the last straw for me, but it's difficult to say if it was more or less perverse than any of his other actions. All I know is that it was just too full of profound and transcendent satisfaction - I could no longer endure his antics. Therefore, I decided that a reaction on my part was required. Whether that reaction was equal and opposite, I'm not so sure. I just felt that some type of balance and decency had to be returned to the world.

Thus, I revealed myself from between the armoire and the wall.

"Okay, motherfucker," I said, while brandishing my wiffle ball bat. "That's quite enough. Get up and step away from the pillow."

Pillow-man stood up and turned to face me instantly. He looked shocked, but perhaps not guilty enough. I suppose it's possible, although unlikely, that he knew I was in the room with him the entire time.

He then crossed his arms - palms on pectorals - like a vampire in a casket.

"Hello there, young lad," he said. "What can I do for you?"

"Oh," I replied, "so that's your game."

"What game do you speak of, son?"

"The game where you're caught doing weird shit and *you* start asking the questions."

"I've never heard of that game. Would you mind telling me the rules?" he asked.

I raised my bat and took a couple steps forward. He remained mummified and tried to de-escalate the situation.

"Now, now. No need to be belligerent," he informed me. "I'm merely curious about this game of yours. I'd like to play, if possible."

"I bet you would."

"Please," he assured me. "I'm genuinely interested. Tell me the rules."

"Well, it goes like this," I began to explain. "First, you tell me what you're doing in my room. Second, you return that bag of hairs by setting it on my bed. Third, you remove yourself from my pool-house and run a minimum of ten miles away from here."

His arms descended from his chest and his hands found their way into his pockets. Obviously, he was trying to display non-threatening body language. He then spoke slowly to me - like I was a child - and carefully enunciated each of his words.

"Okay, sure," he said. "Now that I know the rules, that sounds like a fine game. First things first: My name is Dr. Montgomery Van Cleef, or Dr. Montgomery - as my pubescent and prepubescent patients like to call me. Your mother is a friend of mine and she sent me off on a mission - a mission to find you. As for your hairs, I'd love to place them on your bed, but I simply don't possess them. I also find that to be a rather odd rule for a game. Lastly, in regard to exiting the pool-house, I shall oblige, but I cannot run ten miles away from here. I have a brunch to attend at precisely twelve o'clock, which is in a matter of minutes."

"Who," I asked him, "is my mother? Also, name one item on the brunch menu."

"Why your mother's name is Priscilla Drinkwater and buttermilk beignets, I believe, are to be served before we know it."

"What type of dipping sauce?"

"A salted caramel-maple. My favorite."

"I know you have my hairs in your pocket," I said while moving toward him. "Just show me that you have them and we can call this a draw."

He took a step backward.

"I don't have them," he insisted, "and you'll need a search warrant if you want to see the innards of my pocket."

"Leave them," I demanded once more, "on the bed."

"Okay, well now," he said. "I feel as though we're on good terms, so what I'm going to do is walk by you and head on over to brunch. I'll be sure to tell your mother you'll join us shortly. Goodbye!"

And with that, Dr. Montgomery Van Cleef walked on by me, through the front door, and to the main house.

I decided to let him go unscathed. He would pay for his actions soon enough.

To this day, I still wonder what the degenerate would have done after he smelled my pillow.

Maybe I shouldn't have interrupted.

"Human beings are lucky that we look somewhat visually appealing to one another on the outside. If what's inside of us happened to be on the outside, we'd all be horrified. Our innards are disgusting: the heart, the kidneys, the gall bladder, the brain - all absolutely disgusting. And that's why people are so squeamish and uneasy when they see the slightest bit of blood escape to the surface. It's a sign of who we really are - and it must remain hidden beneath our soft skin."

-Dr. Drinkwater

Munchausen Brunch by Proxy: A Social Duty

———

As LUCK WOULD HAVE IT, I was a wee-bit late for brunch. Sure, I probably could have arrived at high noon, but - somehow or other - I took longer than usual to prink, primp, and preen. For the record, I don't think I was totally conscious of loitering in the pool-house: My tardiness was only semi-passive aggressive - at most. After all, a person needs to care enough to intentionally arrive late. I did so instinctively.

I knew it would be prudent to conduct some surveillance before infiltrating the mid-day festivities. I'm no genius, but I'm also not dumb enough to plunge - willy-nilly - into a potentially hostile social setting. Thankfully, brunch was confined to the sunroom - or the conservatory, as my mother calls it - which enabled me to analyze her guests from around the corner. I was partially obscured by a hutch in the living room, so I'm relatively sure no one could spot me.

Three attendees were present at the time of observation.

My mother - who looked taller and thinner than usual in her pink Chanel boucle suit.

The rotund degenerate, Dr. Montgomery Van Cleef, who opted for a light blue seersucker, a pastel yellow shirt, and a pink bowtie.

And:

The skinny-plump Dr. Phyliss W. Sonnenstein-Schoenboerner, my mother's somewhat new and alarmingly close friend. In terms of garb, she wore a lavender tweed ensemble, an outfit likely influenced by my mother's fashion sense.

The trio was standing in the sunlight by the buffet, chitchatting, and drinking tea. Dr. Van Cleef was the center of attention. His wide-eyed audience listened intently to his words and stirred their tea in a back and forth motion. They alternated between looking fondly at Van Cleef and downward into their cups as they sipped absentmindedly. Their right thumbs and forefingers were pinched around the handles of their teacups, their middle fingers applied below for support. In their left hands were saucers, which hovered beneath their dainty cups - ready to prevent errant drops from reaching the floor.

I scrutinized my subjects for only a minute or so. I probably should have watched them longer, but I couldn't muster the patience to withstand their pretentious ritual for another second. Fact is, I've never witnessed such boring bullshit and I hope I never have to again. Besides, there was no sense in avoiding the inevitable any longer. It was time for me to become part of the painting, and, hopefully, erase myself from it as soon as humanly possible.

If the charade required my participation then 'twere well it were done quickly. After all, I had several non-essential errands on my mind that required immediate attention.

None of the brunch participants took heed of my presence when I slipped into the room. At first, I thought their non-reaction was due to my smooth and graceful entry - a result of light-footed movements and my life-long fear of stomping. When I took my place between the three of them and the buffet table, though, it became clear that something sinister was afoot. Undoubtedly, my appearance must have been noted and their neglect of my existence was premeditated. There was, beyond a reasonable doubt, a method to their rudeness.

Since they were ignoring me - and there was little else to do - I perused the buffet items while the three of them chattered away. I noticed - immediately - that the focus of the table was definitely those buttermilk beignets with salted maple-caramel sauce. All ten of them - along with a miniature pitcher and bowl set - were prominently displayed on a gold-rimmed porcelain serving plate. Next to the flagship dish - to the left - was the crumbled feta quiche Lorraine. To the right, were the parfaits - five in total. The smoked salmon with avocado tartare, however, was suspiciously absent.

I poured some sparkling water from a blue bottle and shifted my concentration to the words floating around me. At the time of my semi-eavesdropping, Dr. Van Cleef was pontificating about tact, manners, and common courtesy. Evidently, he was the victim of a significant social faux pas that left him resentful, peeved, and shaken to the core.

The conversation proceeded as follows:

"Yes, it's true," Dr. Van Cleef demanded.

He took a sip of tea, swallowed, and his cup touched back down on his saucer. He paused briefly for dramatic effect.

"Six couples have already been invited," he continued. "Six couples. And I'm the only husband out of the lot who hasn't received an invitation."

My mother interjected for clarification.

"You mean to say your wife was invited and you weren't?" she inquired.

"Yes, unfortunately, Priscilla, that's exactly what I mean to say."

"Oh, my! There must have been some kind of mix-up," Dr. Sonnenstein-Schoenboerner exclaimed.

"I'm afraid not, Phyliss. I've checked, doubly-double checked, and the reality insists on remaining the same."

My mother dropped a bomb:

"Well, in the interest of full disclosure, Montgomery, Phyliss and I were both invited - along with our husbands."

"Yes, I'm quite aware," answered Dr. Van Cleef instantly, "and I've been wondering since this conversation began when you'd admit that unpleasant truth. I've also heard rumors that some want to add Morty Ballard to the guest list - that insufferable upstart, that deviant fuck."

Dr. Van Cleef took another sip of tea and somewhat hid his face behind his cup. He knew he crossed the line.

My mother and Dr. Sonnenstein-Schoenboerner took half a step back. Their eyebrows shot up and their jaws descended.

Frightened, but thrilled-invigorated, my mother attempted to take the discussion elsewhere.

"That language, Monty!" she said as she tried to find his eyes behind his cup. "I'm surprised at you! Especially since I find Morton to be such an extraordinary gentleman. Not to mention, he's done so, so much for misophonia and misophonia awareness. It's truly astonishing! Until his work, there was - virtually - no effective treatment for misophones. Can you imagine?"

Dr. Sonnenstein-Schoenboerner contributed her two cents.

"Terrible, terrible, terrible," she added. "To go through life tortured by all of the chomping, slurping, and smacking in the world. Thank heavens for geniuses like Morton!"

Dr. Van Cleef was unmoved by their show of support for Morton Ballard. In fact, he raised the level of his argument several steps more.

"As I said, he's a deviant fuck. He always was one, he is one now, and he'll remain one in the future. And mark my words: His secrets will be exposed soon enough."

A discomforting silence pervaded the room.

My mother and Dr. Sonnestein-Schoenboerner were at a loss for their own words, and, accordingly, broke eye-contact with Dr. Van Cleef. Instead, they looked downward at the floor and waited for some type of miraculous relief.

As for myself, I completely turned my back to the group, picked up a bottle of sparkling water, and feigned interest in its label. No calories, no sugar, no sodium.

I wasn't sure what Dr. Van Cleef's next move would be. He successfully backed himself into a corner and his prospects of returning unscathed were anything but promising. But I underestimated him. The resourceful, clever bastard managed to divert attention and deftly revert to his original topic.

"You know what else I've discovered?" he said, with a faint grin on his face. "Somehow or other, my dog walker, George Johnson, also received an invitation to the get-together. How outrageous is that, eh?"

Social suicide, narrowly averted.

My mother and Dr. Sonnenstein-Schoenboerner were jolted back to life. The two chimed in and said "what?" simultaneously. They then smiled at one another, impressed with the fact that they said the same word at the same time.

"You heard correctly," Van Cleef affirmed.

He raised his hands to his neck and his fidgety fingers fine-tuned his bow tie.

"A dog walker, *my dog walker*, was invited to a dinner instead of me. His wife received the nod as well."

"Now that's just mortifying, Monty," my mother replied. "The wife of a dog walker! I must say I just don't know what to tell you. There must be some kind of mis..."

At this precise moment, my mother shifted her attention to me.

"Barry!" she said sharply.

She caught me red-handed. Fatigued by the conversation and in need of nourishment, I'd taken a buttermilk beignet from its gold-rimmed serving dish. I applied some salted maple-caramel sauce - in a swirling motion - and was just about to drop the beignet into my mouth.

"You're not to touch the buttermilk beignets!" she shouted. "*No one* is to touch the buttermilk beignets. Not yet!"

The three of them froze in place and eyeballed me from head to foot with scorn. I guess I did exist after all.

I set the beignet back on the serving dish and my mother provided me with instructions related to its future.

"First of all," she noted, "I can't believe you thought fit to eat that beignet in one bite."

She then pointed at the beignet that received a last minute, temporary reprieve.

"Secondly, please take note: *That* is now *your* beignet. Make sure it is clearly sequestered from the rest. Each guest is allowed two and only two."

"I thought you said I could have three," Dr. Van Cleef interrupted.

My mother transitioned from mildly irritated to a controlled exasperated. Her face was flushed and her eyes angry - her body, otherwise composed.

"No, Monty. Two per guest. You know that. I never said anything but."

There was a brief, but meaningful pause and relaxation of tensions.

My mother brought it to an end before anyone else could.

"Okay, well now," she said, "it looks like our conversation was cut short. Perhaps this is a good opportunity to take our plates and move along to the living room."

Dr. Van Cleef asserted himself quickly and was the first one to the buffet table. Without a second thought, he stepped in front of me and filled his plate with a generous helping of quiche Lorraine, a parfait, two beignets and some sparkling water. Dr. Sonnestein-Schoenboerner followed suit and my mother, in a highly suspicious move, grabbed two plates and filled both of them with the available options. The three of them then disappeared to the living room, leaving me with the remnants of their scavenging. As a matter of course, I took a plate, grabbed the last two beignets, and begrudgingly followed after them.

When I entered the dimly lit - curtains closed - living room, I saw that Drs. Van Cleef and Sonnenstein-Schoenboerner were already seated behind their foldable tray tables. My mother, however, was busy attending to an unidentified man who occupied a leather armchair. He sat with his back to everyone, facing the mantelpiece. For whatever reason, the inconsequential serving scene stood out to me. I remember it in slow motion:

My mother approaches the bald-headed gentleman as cautiously as possible. She lightly presses her left hand to the top of his back, leans over, and whispers something in his right ear. Then, while he remains silent and motionless, she sets his plate on a side table next to the armchair. She's sure to place his food down delicately, as there's already a dirty plate - with salmon remnants - on the table. After that, my mother takes her place next to Dr. Van Cleef on the loveseat.

It's definitely worth noting that it's unclear to me when and how this individual entered the living room. It's also important to note that Darvon, my mother's cat, chose to make an appearance as well. Darvon was at lap height, sleeping next to the loveseat on a pedestal - the second floor of a wicker pet home. Fortunately, the feline was dressed appropriately for brunch and wore a formal affair costume, which consisted of a black coat and a white button-up shirt. Not to be out-done, Darvon also donned a miniature black fedora - with a black and white polka dot hatband - atop his head.

I was just about to eat my first beignet when my mother began to introduce her guests. Her opening remarks seemed well-rehearsed, right down to the way she projected her voice and deliberately articulated her words.

"I would like to begin by thanking all of you for coming today," she said. "I can't tell you how much it means to me that you're part of this conversation, this discussion, this dialogue. As you know, by the end of brunch, I hope to have a better idea of my son's problems, how to treat them, and what he can do to progress properly in this world. Luckily, I have accomplished friends like you - friends who can use their areas of expertise to carefully mold Barry into a competent adult."

My mother placed both of her hands on her knees and looked Drs. Van Cleef and Sonnenstein-Schoenboerner in the eyes, one by one. She was more than excited and so were they. The moment all of them were waiting for had, at last, arrived: It was time for their introductions.

My mother read from several index cards. She began with Dr. Van Cleef.

"The first doctor to introduce today" she announced, "happens to be a clinical psychologist, a theologian, and an economist! He's well-known for his work in regard to reparative therapy, otherwise known as conversion therapy. He's also the author of the lifestyle book *Not Just Human: Furries as Home Companions* and co-author - with Dr. Billingtons - of the bestselling *The Cookie Paid for Itself: Finding God in the Marketplace*. Please extend a warm welcome to none other than Dr. Montgomery Van Cleef!"

My mother and Dr. Sonnenstein-Schoenboerner eagerly clapped. Dr. Van Cleef, with a smug smile on his face, added to the applause with a clap or two.

"Now to introduce our second doctor!" my mother continued. "This doctor earned her Ph.D. in Physiology, but switched pathways after ten years. Now, she's the most popular and successful family counselor in the town of Needles and, quite possibly, all of Massachusetts. In addition, she's a self-help guru and the author of *Social Cues: For Me and For You*, a personal awareness book for children. Currently, she is the president of the Foundation for Internal Healing and Discovery, which devotes itself to all forms of acceptable love and intimacy in today's modern world. Let's give it up for Dr. Phyliss W. Sonnenstein-Schoenboerner!"

Additional muted clapping ensued.

"Lastly," my mother said, "I'd like to take a moment to present an extra special guest - a guest who somehow found time out of his busy schedule to grace us with his presence today.

"He, of course, is not your ordinary MD. Instead, he is a Medical Renaissance Man (MRM). He happens to be a Doctor of Podiatric Medicine, Veterinary Medicine, Psychiatry, and Dentistry. He's most famous, however, for his work as Psychiatrist-in-Chief at Needles General Hospital.

"Most recently, he authored the widely-read article *Shoaling, Schooling, and the Oddity Effect: The Impact of Compulsory Public Education on American Social Patterns*. In addition, he's the man behind the creation of The JoJo Juniper Center for Unlikeable Children. JoJo's tragic murder hurt him dearly and served as the impetus for its formation. The ribbon cutting ceremony will be in December.

"Please welcome our very own Dr. Orval Billingtons!"

The clapping session for Dr. Billingtons was more intense and persisted longer the than previous applause for Drs. Van Cleef and Sonnenstein-Schoenboerner. The three of them seemed to worship Dr. Billingtons, but, at the same time, feared ending his ovation too quickly. As for Dr. Billingtons himself, I couldn't tell if he listened to a single word that was said about him. The doctor still had his back to us and appeared to be focused on his share of quiche Lorraine.

Eventually, after a minute or so, the palm slapping came to an end. Unfortunately for me, though, its cessation signaled the beginning of my interrogation.

My mother initiated the intervention.

"Well, now," she said. "Looks like we've got all of our ducks in a row, so let's get started, shall we?"

Dr. Van Cleef blotted his mouth after eating some quiche and assumed control.

"Barry," he said, sternly. "I'm going to cut right to the chase: We think you are a troubled, young bird. As a result, we've convened here today to mend your wings, so you can take flight once again."

"My wings are just fine, thanks."

"On the contrary," countered Dr. Sonnenstein-Schoenboerner. "They're anything but fine. Please, there's no time for denial."

My mother re-focused the conversation.

"Do you know why you're here today, Barry?" she inquired.

I answered as truthfully as possible.

"I came for the beignets," I told her. "I received a brunch invitation not long ago that specifically noted beignets would be on the menu. That's why I'm here. Solely for the beignets. Although I should say the sparkling water is better than I thought it would be. The conversation, however, is a bit dry."

My mother, Dr. Van Cleef, and Dr. Sonnenstein-Schoenboerner each attempted to reprimand me at the same time. Dr. Sonnestein-Schoenboerner reigned supreme after a brief struggle.

"I feel as though you're not getting it, young man," she informed me. "You're here for a reason. You are, as Dr. Van Cleef said, a troubled, frail, and directionless bird. And we're here to get to the root of your malfunction. Pull it straight from where it grows. So, let me ask you a simple question: What do you think your greatest problem is?"

I took my time before I responded, which prompted my adversaries to lean toward me a bit. Shockingly, they actually thought I'd answer the question.

"Okay, Dr. Sonnenstein-Schoenboerner," I said. "Despite that fact you inserted frail and directionless to Dr. Montgomery's bird comparison, I'm going to answer you. But, before I do, I'd like to take this opportunity to thank my mother for preparing such an extraordinary brunch. You really cobbled together quite the spread, and I thank you for your efforts."

I looked toward my less-than-pleased mother and she muttered "That's kind of you to say, Barry."

Dr. Van Cleef piped up.

"You're deflecting, Barry. It's quite clear you're deflecting. Be a good lad and answer Dr. Sonnenstein-Schoenboerner."

"Sure, Dr. Montgomery. You're the boss. The truth is, I'm not really sure what my *greatest* problem is. But, if I had to venture a guess, I'd say parking tickets is up there."

My mother was displeased and looked at me incredulously.

"Parking tickets, Barry?" she asked. "You can't be serious."

She and her friends settled back into their seats.

"Yes, parking tickets. That's what I said."

Dr. Sonnenstein-Schoenboerner was already fed up with me.

"How on earth," she said, "could *parking* tickets be your greatest problem?"

Her voice accentuated the par of parking.

"Well, thank you for asking, Dr. Sonnenstein-Schoenboerner. The truth is I've been getting them in my sleep. Recently, come to think of it, I've received more than usual in my dreams. I can't understand it. It happens to me no matter what. Sometimes the meters are broken. Sometimes I'm legally parked and return within the allotted time. Still, when I get to my car, I find these orange citations plastered all over my windshield. It seems unavoidable."

Dr. Van Cleef appeared more interested than the other two.

"Do you contest the tickets?" he inquired. "I would contest the tickets, if I were you."

"That's a great question, Dr. Montgomery. And, as a matter of fact, I do contest the tickets - if my dreams last long enough. I've gone so far as to hire some of the best traffic ticket lawyers my imagination has to offer, but to no avail. I either show up late to my hearing and lose by default, or the judge defies logic and finds me responsible."

"At least it's not a moving violation," Dr. Van Cleef, the optimist, added. "If that were the case, your car insurance would skyrocket. You might even lose your license to operate vehicles in your dreams."

"Okay, okay. Enough of this nonsense," said Dr. Sonnenstein-Schoenboerner. "Don't indulge him."

"I'm merely trying to get the subject to elab..."

My mother cut Dr. Van Cleef off with authority.

"What we have here," she explained, "is an alexithymic - among several other diagnoses - which is what both of you have told me in past discussions about him. His dreams are mundane and he lacks the ability to express himself emotionally. Are you aware of alexithymia, Barry?"

"It's the disorder from which I suffer," I agreed. "Clearly. I coincide with both of those extremely general symptoms. I guess, relatively speaking, it's not as bad as being a trichophiliac. I'd be really fucked up if that were the case."

"Barry! Language! Your language is terrible," my mother said. "Besides, what is a trichophiliac? That sounds disgusting!"

"I just looked it up in the dictionary before I got here," I said, "but I think a noted doctor, such as Dr. Montgomery, would be better equipped to explain trichophilia than me."

"Hair fetishism," stated Dr. Montgomery in a grave tone. "Trichophiliacs find hair to be sexually arousing. Titillating, one might say."

I jumped in to maximize concern.

"You'd be surprised" I noted, "who is afflicted with trichophilia. Could even be the person sitting next to you."

My mother looked horrified. Dr. Van Cleef moved to quell her fears.

"Less than ten percent, Barry," he said. "I'd say less than ten percent of people are trichophiliacs."

"Somehow, despite those odds, I feel like there's a trichophil-iac in the room," I warned everyone. "They say males are more likely to be trichophiliacs."

Dr. Sonnenstein-Schoenboerner re-entered the discourse.

"I'd like to remind everyone that we are here to straighten out Barry. We are, once again, losing focus."

"That's correct, Phyliss," my mother concurred. "Let's get right back to it. Barry, let me ask you this: What happened to that girlfriend of yours?"

"I'm not really sure. I haven't see her in some time. I guess things petered out and came to an end."

Dr. Sonnenstein-Schoenboerner appeared worked up.

"Is it because she wasn't satisfied with you?" she asked defi-antly. "Is that what it was?"

"You'd have to ask her."

"I've been told you haven't been in a relationship with a female for a great deal of time," she continued. "Do you think the reason for that is because - among several other things - that you're gay, Barry?"

"No, I don't believe that I'm gay. At least not at this moment in time."

"Sounds like a gay answer to me," said Dr. Van Cleef. "You know, I'd say his condition is the result of the lack of father-son bonding during Barry's childhood. Phyliss, your foundation, the one for Internal Healing and Discovery, suggests aversive mea-sures to be taken, doesn't it?"

"Yes, Monty. That's correct. We've found that tickling - aversive tickling - can bring about catharsis in wayward gay youths.

Their toxic emotions are released, their souls are purged, and epiphanies reached."

"I'd be happy to carry out the aversive tickling," suggested Dr. Van Cleef. "In fact, I'll do it right now, if the rest of you feel that's necessary. I could also meet privately with Barry later on tonight. Whatever the group thinks is best for his welfare."

This proposal caused me to respond.

"I don't think that will be necessary, Dr. Montgomery. But - out of curiosity, and logistically speaking - how would you go about tickling me?"

Dr. Sonnenstein-Schoenboerner tackled this question.

"You will be placed face up across his lap and he will tickle you until you reach catharsis," she revealed. "While tickling, he'll repeat gentle and compassionate words, phrases, and ideas. He will communicate to you what you should have been told as a child."

"Whatever it takes," my mother said. "I just want Barry to be more like his brother, Gerry. That's all I ask for, that's all I want."

These comments prompted me to ask my mother a question or two.

"Do you think it's possible," I said, "that you're projecting your own problems onto me? After all, you've always enjoyed making someone else's tragedy your own. Why not try to make me miserable as well?"

"Absolutely not, Barry. That's ridiculous and insulting."

I pointed at Darvon.

"For instance," I told my mother, "look at that right there. It doesn't need to wear - or want to wear - a sport coat, shirt, and a fedora."

My mother sat straight up from the loveseat and threw her pointer finger at me.

"It! It, Barry! Respect the cat's identity! Darvon has a name and that name is Darvon! As you well know, he loves to wear his costumes and hats. He also catches cold when he isn't properly dressed. You know he gets the chills."

"Does anything else plague Darvon - besides the chills?"

My mother seemed to calm down and took her seat. She likes talking about Darvon's infirmities.

"Well, he has multiple food allergies," my mother elaborated. "He also can't be anywhere near swordfish, strawberries, corn on the cob, spicy tuna rolls, poached eggs, or partly skimmed milks."

"What else? Any other afflictions?"

"He has his migraines and fevers as well."

"Is that it?"

"Okay, fine. He battles with restless leg syndrome, narcolepsy, and sleep apnea. Not to mention, he had a seizure during the night last Wednesday."

"Are you sure he has all of these problems?"

Dr. Sonnenstein-Schoenboerner attempted to stop the interrogation.

"I don't believe," she insisted, "this line of questioning is necessary or prod..."

My mother, however, could not be deterred.

"The vet, Barry! The vet confirmed all of this!"

"I don't know. I'm not so sure, Mother. You're either making his symptoms up or Darvon is malingering. One or the other."

The thought of Darvon as a malingerer was too much for my mother. In response, she pursued a tactic I didn't expect. She put her hands to her face - as if to block her head from something or other - and started to say the same words over and over.

"Oh, my! Oh, my, my, my," she wailed. "He's doing it again! He's doing it again! Oh, my! Oh, my, my, my!"

Drs. Van Cleef and Sonnenstein-Schoenboerner rose from their seats to provide assistance.

Dr. Van Cleef spoke up first.

"What's he doing, Priscilla? Tell us what he's doing and we won't let him get away with it."

"That's right, Priscilla," Dr. Sonnenstein-Schoenboerner added. "Just tell us what he's doing and we'll take care of you."

"He's trying to read my mind!" my mother cried. "I can feel him trying to get in there! He's wants to get in there and control my mind!"

"Oh, shit!" Dr. Van Cleef said. "Psychotronics! I wasn't sure about it earlier, but now I know better. The boy was trying that with me, too!"

I don't like to be falsely accused, so I attempted to transfer blame.

"How do you know it's me trying to wash your brains?" I asked. "It's probably Darvon the malingerer. He's attempting to tell you that he's overweight and he'd like to get outside for some fresh air and exercise. He's also afraid one of you wants to tickle the shit out of him."

The thought of Darvon as a malingerer and a reader of minds was too much for my mother. She jumped to her feet, and with

Drs. Van Cleef and Sonnenstein-Schoenboerner surrounding her, picked up Darvon. Then, the three of them hastily exited the living room.

Fortunately, they didn't return.

The room was relatively silent.

Except, of course, for Dr. Billingtons. I had forgotten about him.

The absence of my mother and her doctor friends brought him to my attention once again.

It was just the two of us.

I looked over at him - at his back and his head - and watched as he finished his parfait. He took one last bite from his spoon. Then, he set the nearly empty parfait glass on the side table next to him. He clasped his hands together on his lap and remained in that position until I left.

He didn't say a word or move an inch.

I considered saying something to him.

But I didn't.

Instead, I retreated to the pool-house. I needed to organize my thoughts and figure out how to proceed with the remainder of the day.

"I remember wearing chambray before I was old enough to remember wearing chambray."

"Sometimes chambray is in style. Sometimes it's out of style. *Now*, you ask? I can't honestly say where chambray stands *now*, but I can tell you that I don't give a fuck."

"Cotton, linen, lightweight, white weft, colorful warp. Sometimes gingham, sometimes solid, but always perfect - on me, at least."

"As far as I know, chambray shirts are named after the Chevalier d'Eon Chambray. He was a spy, a war hero, a woman, a novelist, and a fencing instructor at Leiden University. He's famous for leading the Charge of the Foggy Night Crusade. There are at least two regions in France named after him."

-WAYNE

Snippets regarding chambray shirts, why he wears them exclusively, and the history of the garment (collected over a one-month period)

Banished

———

FOR SOME REASON - PERHAPS because it was Columbus Day - I decided that I should return to the House of Wayne, also known as Spit House. The truth is, I hadn't heard from Wayne in a long time, not even by way of fax, his preferred mode of communication. I wasn't so much worried about the Patron-Saint-of-Hare-Brained-Schemes, but curious as to what kind of intrigue in which he was then immersed. I sent a fax to announce my intent to visit, but received no reply. I decided to drop in on him nevertheless.

To my surprise, Wayne was the only one home that afternoon. I knocked on the front door and waited a couple of minutes for him to respond. When he finally did, he opened up the mail slot and instructed me to "pass ten dollars of collateral through the slot."

Apparently, he needed a way to validate the seriousness of my non-appointment. Foolishly, I passed the ten dollars to him.

He continued with his instructions.

"Now," he said, "if you could be so kind, please kneel down so I can see your face for positive-identification-security-purposes."

"You know it's me," I replied. "You can hear my voice."

"I have reason to believe a tape recording of your voice was leaked and fell into the wrong hands. Do not take offense. This is a matter of policy."

"How long has this policy been in place?"

"I'm sorry," he said, "but I am not at liberty to provide that information."

"Why don't you go around to the window and take a look at me."

"I can't," he insisted. "Once the transaction begins, it's against policy to interrupt its progress. Besides, we've chewed off more than can bite us at this point. Kneel down and show me your face, please."

"No, thanks. I'm going to pass on this one. If you could be so kind as to pass my ten dollars back."

"That was collateral, asshole. This kind of attitude is exactly why the collateral policy was instituted."

"I'm going to need that money back," I demanded.

"Again, and for the last time: I'm sorry, but that won't be possible. You can't reverse the curse."

"I think you mean I can't reverse course."

"No, Barry," he said. "I know exactly what I mean and that's definitely not it. Are you going to kneel down or what?"

"This is total bull-shit. I'll kneel down, but don't do any bizarre shit to my face."

Against my better judgment, I acquiesced to Wayne's peculiar demand and knelt down before the mail slot. To my amazement, Wayne didn't take advantage of the situation – he truly wanted to be sure that I stood on the opposite side of the door. Then again, I suppose it's also possible that sick bastard wanted me to assume a dutiful, servile position. Regardless, he didn't spray my face with Windex, chemical, or any other potentially blinding substances.

After a minute or so, Wayne unlocked and opened the front door. I must have successfully passed the entrance ritual.

He then apologized for the delay, and said that he had been "preparing his breakfast," and, therefore, did not hear me knocking. This explanation was unexpected, seeing as though the kitchen is within twelve feet of the front door. However, that gap in logic was quickly accounted for when Wayne opened the cellar door.

He turned to face me.

"Please," he said, "won't you follow me downstairs?"

When I reached the basement I saw that a table and three chairs had been set up next to the boiler. One of the chairs was occupied by a red, full-size, Teletubby costume – an outfit Wayne often donned in order to frighten teenage vandals at Needles State Psychiatric Hospital. The other two seats were vacant. I noticed the table had been meticulously set, complete with a fine-white-table-cloth, placemats, silverware, and an assortment of jellies and jams. On one of the plates, sat a piece of immaculately burnt toast.

I also noticed that Wayne had, once again, written his name in some dust on the side of the boiler.

Anyhow, Wayne graciously offered me a seat and sat down in front of the plate which held the still-smoking, charred toast. He looked harried, his hair was disheveled, and his sweatshirt was inside-out. He didn't appear well – to say the least. I figured his home-life wasn't exactly in its prime. It seemed beyond a reasonable doubt that his family banished him to the basement.

At first, he said nothing. I just sat there and watched as he spread a healthy amount of apple jelly onto his carcinogenic-carbon-coated-slice-of-toast. When he finished spreading the jelly, he carved up the toast into several pieces of equal size - approximately one inch squared - and began to slowly and methodically eat them, one by one, left to right, from the bottom to the top of the slice.

While he ate, I posed some logical questions.

"Have you been exiled here?" I asked. "This basement is unfinished and kind of dark and dank."

He appeared miffed at the question as he chewed on a small piece of toast.

"That's utter nonsense, Barry, and frankly, I'm insulted that you would say such a thing," he retorted while looking in the opposite direction.

Although I could plainly see a pillow and a sleeping bag laid out on the floor next to the furnace, I decided to move on to my next question.

"Do you think," I said, "it's a good idea to devour such thoroughly burnt toast?"

He shifted his head toward mine and look downright angry.

"That's very ignorant, Barry," he said. "Very ignorant. Do you mean to say you know nothing, absolutely nothing, about the perils of eating lightly toasted bread? Toast must be well-done. Well-*well*-done. I find it hard to believe that no one has told you well-done toast with apple jelly is the greatest, safest breakfast in the world. Are you completely unawares?"

He then suggested I try some, but I chose to decline his generous proposition. He also offered the Red-Tele-Tubby some of his toast, but Stinky-Winky remained aloof and quiet.

His silence was understood as rejection.

"Whoever grapples with the cookie monster
should see to it that in the process he
doesn't wind up covered in crumbs."

"You may gaze longingly into the dark hole of a
strawberry frosted doughnut, but remember - it stares,
in devious wonder, straight back into your soul.

"And don't forget, soon after you eat that pink
pastry, it will appear in one of your dreams
and ask a simple question: When do you think
you'll become what you've devoured?"

-DR. DRINKWATER

Selected pearls of wisdom delivered
to Barry as a toddler

Bingo Bilocation

———◆———

AFTER SITTING NEXT TO THE boiler and Stinky-Winky for a while, Wayne decided to take a somber walk down memory lane. It must have been the sight of the furnace that inspired his forlorn flashback. He stared straight at it instead of me, and recounted a major injustice he endured while in elementary school – an occurrence he termed "The Bingo Bilocation Incident."

Wayne related the story to me in a growly, grouchy tone. He jumped right to it with no introduction.

"I'll never forget that Friday afternoon my fourth grade class played bingo," he said. "I'll never forget that crime against me - a young, tender, eleven-and-a-half-year-old pupil. And I'm going to tell you all about it. You're going to hear the truth, the half-truth, the whole truth, and nothing but the truth - straight from the horse's mouth, as you like to say.

"So, to make a short story long, let me begin by telling you this: I just needed to fill in one more space to win – that goddamned O-Sixty-Nine. And that's when I bilocated. Yep, that's when I bilocated for the first time in my life."

"What does bilocated mean again?" I asked Wayne.

"Please refrain from interrupting," Wayne angrily replied. "All will be answered organically as the tale develops."

"I'm sorry for the interruption," I said.

"You just interrupted again, you uncouth fuck. What don't you understand? If you interrupt a third time, I will cancel story time."

Despite the fact that I wanted to bash Wayne's brains in, I repressed my violent thoughts, played along, and said nothing.

"As I was saying," he continued, "before some rude *ASS*-hole interrupted me, I never won when we played bingo. I never even came close. We must have played a thousand times in school. And you'd think I'd come close to winning at least once. But no, you would be dead wrong. I was always shit-out-of-luck when it came to bingo.

Except one time - the last time I was permitted to play.

"I remember sitting there at my desk, behind Samantha Coleman, thinking really hard about Sister Mary calling out that letter-number combination. And then, somehow, some way, one-half of me happened to *POP* forward in time. Yes, you heard right: I found myself occupying the present and the future simultaneously. It was slightly confusing, but I'm confident that I can accurately remember the future I stepped into that day.

"I heard Sister Mary call out '**OOOO-Sixty-Nine, OOOO-Sixty-Nine**,' so I placed my chip on that spot, yelled 'bingo!' and walked to the front of the room to collect my prize. It was during this moment – as I held out my hand to receive a brand new St. Paul the Apostle prayer card – that my mind was beset by an uncomfortable fuzzy-kind-of-feeling. I lost track of time paths, my bearings were totally scrambled. I was dizzied - I was dazed.

"Next thing I knew, I looked down at my card and noticed I hadn't filled in **O-Sixty-Nine** with my bingo chip. Without thinking, I yelled out 'bingo!' again and walked toward Sister Mary.

"In less than a second, I discovered that I made a mistake – the present had yet to catch up with the future.

"Every kid in class looked at me as if I had lost my mind. Sister Mary stopped me in my tracks and stared me down.

'Wayne,' she said, 'you naughty, presumptuous, incorrigible, little fool! I've yet to call out the winning number. Sit your precocious-self back down immediately!'

"I passionately retorted, 'Yes, you did! It's **OOOO-Sixty-Nine**! Just check the number in the palm of your hand!'

"She looked down at her hand, opened her fist, and sure enough, there it was:

O-Sixty-Nine.

"I thought I had been vindicated, but Sister Mary was of a different opinion. She was spiteful and full of wrath.

'You've cheated, you little scoundrel,' she yelled at the top of her scratchy voice. 'Quite clearly, you're in league with the devil, aren't you? Now, if you value Jesus and Mary you're going to explain to me - rationally and immediately - exactly how you did that. And, if you can't, I'm going to consider you to be one of Satan's disciples. Do you understand that? One of Satan's dirty, degenerate, depraved disciples.'

"I had no answer for her. I knew I'd better keep the dog in the bag and tell the cat not to lie in its sleep. In other words, I knew the truth would have been worse than silence and I couldn't come up with an alternative story. So I froze. I froze in my tracks and said nothing.

And bingo!

"That's when she informed me that I had to be punished for my sin, for my use of the **Black Bingo Arts**.

My penalty was severe.

"I was instructed to carry a large wooden trunk down to the basement, place myself inside of it, and await my appointment with the 'Abomination of Desolation.' I was advised - required - to remain patient in the trunk for a long time. The custodian, Mr. Chase, was going to come down at the end of the day and throw the trunk, with me inside, into the roaring furnace.

'If you burn,' Sister Mary added, 'then we'll know you're merely a disturbed young man, not the devil himself.'

"Because I was a dutiful student, I carried that trunk down to the basement, got inside of it, and prepared myself to meet head-on with the Abomination of Desolation. Yes, I waited to be incinerated – meekly and faithfully, for the rest of the school day, a total of three-and-a-half-hours.

"My combustion that day, obviously, never happened. Just before the dismissal bell rang, Sister Mary, the-good-bride-of-Christ, sent her favorite little suck-up and minion, the craven Calvin Turlington, down to the boiler room. That sniveling-little-coward opened the lid to my chest and told me I had been granted mercy – a last minute pardon.

'Wayne,' Calvin said, 'Sister Mary says it's time for you to emerge from darkness. You may come out from that box, but only if you promise to carry it back to our classroom and recite sixty-nine Hail Marys.'

"So, yeah, I promised Calvin I would lug that forsaken box all the way back to class and recite, as commanded, the sixty-nine Hail Marys. Yes, I agreed to these terms - albeit not without some reservations - and carried the trunk up the stairs and back to class. I then walked home – after saying three-and-a-half Hail Marys."

At this point, it seemed as if Wayne had finished unraveling his yarn. I was about to ask him some follow-up questions, but I was immediately enjoined to cease and desist. He finally quit his earnest eyeballing of the furnace and looked me in the face.

"Well," he said, "that concludes the story of my first bilocation, as well as my breakfast. If you don't mind, I have something else of unparalleled importance to tell you. However, I cannot tell you here – it's far too dangerous. There are spies everywhere. Please accompany me to the Crown Victoria."

"Several years ago, as I was looking from out my attic window, I saw a large bird, a kumquat perhaps, or maybe a cockatoo, one or the other, soaring majestically through the blue afternoon sky. Suddenly, a small sparrow, or chickadee of some sort, appeared out of the heavens and landed directly upon the kumquat's back. That tiny bird started to ride on that kumquat, like a passenger, reminiscent of Jonas and the whale. It was a beautiful moment and a miracle to witness - to see those birds working together so harmoniously. I remember I said to myself, 'Now *that's* symbiosis if I've ever seen it. *That's* nature in all its glory.'"

-WAYNE

A temporary naturalist

CHAPTER 16A

Doomsday is a Tuesday

———————

ONCE AGAIN, I FOUND MYSELF sitting next to Wayne in the Crown Victoria's passenger seat – and, once again, he was driving like an absolute maniac. This time, however, his frantic driving was nicely offset by the singular tranquility of that particular afternoon. It was surprisingly pleasant outside, about dusk, the roads – devoid of traffic. The sun was setting slowly and the clouds, with the help of some smog, created a never-ending, phantom-like, purple and orange horizon. It was perfectly quiet outside – I don't think I heard a single car horn, police sirens, or any hostile music polluting the air.

Despite these idyllic conditions, Wayne had the windows of the Crown Victoria rolled up tightly. He was blasting Bach – one of his dreary, yet sedating organ preludes – at full volume, which was unexpected. I never knew he liked Bach, or that he even knew of the composer. Although, he did name that monkey of his after a cryptic melodist named Choppinwood, a figure who may or may not have existed. Nevertheless, I assumed that he was blaring the prelude at such elevated decibels in order to disguise any discussion we might have en route to the unknown. I'm sure he believed there were microphones planted in the car and his privacy was in jeopardy.

Clearly, it was rather unclear exactly what Wayne communicated to me on that car ride. The volume of the music was truly deafening and I could only make out jumbled bits and pieces here and there. Still, at the beginning, it sounded as if he made some of his standard statements and asked his regular questions. I'm relatively certain he said something about how he hadn't seen my girlfriend "in what seems like forever" and inquired as to why I was still wearing a full suit. I attempted to respond, but I knew all-too-well that even if he could hear me, he still wouldn't be listening, or at least care enough to register my replies. Therefore, I resorted to mouthing some nonsense words, which he, oddly enough, acted as if he understood completely.

For the most part, however, he seemed to focus on the need to prepare for the end of the world. He blabbed about Sister Mary again – his favorite, former, personal sadist – and some gobble-dygook to the tune of Doomsday. I suppose, despite the torture she inflicted upon Wayne, Sister Mary had somehow made him believe she was right about one prediction - Doomsday is on its way and it's scheduled for a Tuesday.

I'm relatively sure that's what Wayne communicated to me in the car. I remember he once mentioned how much sinister Sister Mary thoroughly enjoyed telling children about the upcoming apocalypse. She often told Wayne and his friends that Doomsday was on the horizon and that it was due to strike on a Tuesday during their afternoon recess. She even added that it would probably happen while playing four-square. There would be a box for each horseman.

Apparently, the grim, evil seed Sister Mary planted inside Wayne's skull had finally taken root in a way she could never have predicted. Granted, my comprehension may have been compromised, but for the remainder of that car ride, Wayne went on about his discovery of "a path to righteousness" and the importance of the "meek prevailing" – an idea he made sure to explain to me and acted as if he invented. At one point, he began to vigorously gesticulate-pontificate and claimed he had "repented" and "atoned" for his "grievous, sinful past." He also notified me that he was "turning to a true" and was inches away from achieving "total salvation." Finally, he divulged that he was stockpiling "non-perishables" such as "Devil-Dogs and Rice-Krispie-Treats," so his family could survive in great abundance post-Armageddon.

Of particular note, right before he turned the dial to eliminate the prelude, he said something about sin-eaters and a sighting of the Mothman. Unsurprisingly, when I attempted to interrogate him about these subjects, he put his pointer finger in front of his lips.

"Not now," he commanded, "respect the dead."

At that instant, he shut the music off in the car and whipped through the gates of Needles Cemetery.

"It's better to shear a pin than blow an engine. That's why I always store some extra pins in the garage."

-DR. DRINKWATER

On the Path to Salvation

———

As Wayne zig-zagged the Crown Victoria through a maze of obelisks, wrought iron fences, and headstones, it appeared as though he hadn't the faintest idea where he was headed. In fact, I'm fairly certain that we drove past one particular statue – a dog covered with a blanket, sitting atop a stone pedestal – at least three times. Then again, his haphazard cemetery driving may have been intentional, done to lose his numerous, non-existent pursuers.

After about ten minutes of either punctilious or devil-may-care-driving, Wayne pulled off to the side and parked beneath a massive, gnarled oak tree. Then, randomly and without saying a word, he leapt out of the car, slammed the door, and made off toward the edge of a shadowy hollow. I figured that he intended for me to follow, so I took off after him in sluggish, luke-warm pursuit.

I was half-way down Ivy Path - not far from Primrose Path - when I heard the words "I'm overrrrrr herrrrrre, shiiiiiiiiiit-heaaaaaaaaaaaad" ghoulishly reverberate through the twilight air. When I looked for the source of that eloquent proclamation, I spotted Wayne's silhouetted figure. He was sitting on some stone steps, next to a vault, on the side of a hill.

Within a minute, I found myself perched beside him, gazing upon the bottom of a glen. Beneath us were two weeping beech trees, hunched-over-looking a small pond. Below the trees, were several gravestones that poked out here and there from amidst leafy, cascading branches - they looked like teeth. For a moment, I thought I was having an attack of the déjà-vus, but then it dawned on me: I had visited this place before – the last time I saw my girlfriend. I once stood with her beneath those very beech trees.

Per usual, Wayne quickly interrupted, and my flashback was put on hold indefinitely. With a solemn, inquisitive expression on his face, he copied the angle of my glare and looked toward the trees.

"This is my favorite vault," he said. "Vault number 574. There's just something about it, something I can't quite put my finger on. Perhaps it's the view. Perhaps it's what lies beneath. But listen, now is the time to tell you something of great importance. Something I can only explain to someone I absolutely trust. Something that must be said before the Mothman cometh. And I'm going to tell you everything - the whole kitten caboodle."

"I started with English. And, as soon as I mastered it, I began to study Pig Latin. But I figure I may as well be up-front about it: I don't understand how it works. I've been trying to decipher that language for years, but, at this point, I've decided it's just not in the cards for me. I'm never going to crack the code."

-WAYNE

Reflecting on his efforts to become a multi-linguist

Traveling in the Breakdown Lane is Strictly Prohibited: Objects in the Mirror are Closer than they Appear

———◆———

WAYNE LAUNCHED INTO HIS ENIGMATIC story about **Exit Thirty-Three B** before I knew it. I wanted to interrupt him right away, but somehow I resisted the urge. After all, there's nothing like twilight story-time in a cemetery.

"Not long ago," Wayne began, "I was driving home on the highway, Route 128, when I noticed the arrow on my gas gauge was pointing at empty. Yes, it's true, I've driven on a drained tank many times before and I've never run out of gas. This time, though, I had been operating on fumes for too long. When my car started to put-sputtery-put, I realized I wasn't going to make it any farther. So, I pulled off to the side of the road and into the breakdown lane. I got out of my car, opened the trunk to grab a red emergency gas tank, and began my journey to the closest highway off-ramp.

"What seemed so close was actually far away. The sun was baking-hot and I immediately began to sweat profusely. I felt like

I was a nomad making my way across the desert. The side of the road resembled a wasteland, loaded with dirt, dust, sand, shards of glass – festooned by highway-goers with cigarette butts, plastic wrappers and scratched lottery tickets. Not a drop of water was in sight, except for deceptive mirages. They looked like skinny rivers that crossed the lanes of the highway ahead of me, and they disappeared, one by one, before I could reach them.

"I felt like I was walking in slow motion compared to the cars that screamed, whizzed, zoomed by me at incredible speeds. But I was at their mercy. I didn't want to end up like the bloody, mangled road-kill strewn here and there along my path. I remember looking at their frightened faces, forever frozen by the sudden-death that snatched their souls from this world. But the dead kept me in my place, reminded me to steer clear, to avoid standing in the way of the never-ending progression of automobiles.

"Anyhow, my morale was at an all-time-low when I first caught sight of an off-ramp in the distance. Quite honestly, I'm fairly certain I was about to pass out due to heat exhaustion. But then I was revived – revived the moment I laid my eyes upon a sign in the distance. Yes, something began to stir inside of me as soon as I discerned that magical number letter combination – **Thirty-Three B**."

CHAPTER 17

Exit Thirty-Three B

———

"FROM ABOVE – AN AERIAL view – or on a map," Wayne continued, "I'm sure **Exit Thirty-Three B** looks like it's just part of the stereotypical cloverleaf interchange. But I assure you, as I walked along the edge of that off-ramp, I found that **Exit Thirty-Three B** is most unusual-peculiar. I've taken that exit many times and often marveled at the small circular forest it encompasses. Obviously, driving a car at such inhuman speeds, I've never really had the opportunity to investigate. But this time was different. I was on foot. And as my curiosity pushed me toward that uncommon detour, I also felt pulled - pulled by some kind of invisible force.

"At first, I didn't think it would take much time to explore, but when I crossed through the litter and brush that lined the periphery, it became clear that the enclosed forest is much larger than I anticipated. Soon enough, I found myself standing in front of a maze of pine trees that extended as far as I could see. As I walked deeper and deeper within the pine forest, the sounds of all those cars rushing forward, inching toward a million different artificial deadlines, began to subside. Eventually, I couldn't hear any automobiles at all.

"Pine trees towered over me and in all directions. It was easy to walk amongst them though – all lack branches until midway up their trunks. From that point, the live branches begin and eventually form an impressive pine needle canopy. Only bits and pieces of the sky can be seen from the ground. I'm sure next-to-nothing can be seen from above the tree tops.

"The terrain inside of **Exit Thirty-Three B** is carpeted with millions, possibly billions, of orange pine needles. All of those needles, working in collusion, rendered my footsteps completely silent as I walked upon that cushiony-soft landscape. It was clear that each of my muted steps forward brought me closer and closer to something of great importance. I was sure that I wouldn't be able to retrace my tracks. Still, I wasn't in the least bit concerned. I felt totally free and at peace. I was too curious to even entertain a thought that would hold me back.

"After wandering aimlessly for what seemed like an eternity, I thought I saw something move and quickly disappear behind a pine tree. Whatever it was, it looked like it may have been furry, possibly made out of cotton-candy. I walked in the direction of this wondrous, perplexing sight and came upon something I have never witnessed, or, for that matter, even knew existed. Yes, right there, below me in a large glacial hole, was a disorderly flock of sheep, fifteen or so, jogging haphazardly – one was actually climbing a tree – in all directions. And when I say sheep, I mean the type of sheep with which the two of us are familiar. The only difference was these sheep weren't domesticated. They were autonomous and free, seemingly without a shepherd to guide them.

"I soon found myself making my way toward the bottom of that mystical glacial hole. It's funny, I can't remember the last time I felt so happy. I mean, I was in irregularly high spirits when I descended the side of that bowl. It's not every day one sees undomesticated sheep frolicking in the forest, and that sight brought out the best in me. Thing is, though, by the time I got to the bottom, all of the sheep had somehow vanished. I don't know where they went, but they were gone. I stumbled onward and tried to locate them, but to no avail. I think it's possible they may have evaporated.

"That's when I bumped right smack into a massive copper beech tree. I don't know how to explain it, but somehow I neglected to notice it before we made contact. Perhaps it materialized after the sheep so rudely disappeared. I'm not sure. Considering the never-ending maze of pines, it's somewhat disconcerting that a tree of that magnitude could sneak up on me. Now that I think about it, that beech should have stuck out like your mother, chewing a ripe and juicy plum.

"Oh, but before I go on, I should mention that at about the time I became aware of that beech, I noticed I was standing in the midst of an outcropping of archaic ruins. Yes, I seemed to be in the center of an inexact circle of crumbling columns. Some of the columns looked to be about fifteen feet in height, others half that size, some only a quarter. In addition, scattered among the pine needles, were gray, granite-looking stones that either served as markers or were part of a foundation at one time. Most mysterious-queer, however, was a gigantic, granite human head set on its side. It looked like it was trying to listen to whispers from the earth. The chiseled man's face looked concerned, but also had this flat, unnatural, yet dream-like, smile.

Anyhow, back to where I was.

"That copper beech really caught my attention. It's true, I may have been somewhat groggy and overtired, but that tree seemed to emit this extra special, ignis-fatuus-kind-of-glow. Not to mention, its limbs were downright monstrous in both length and width. The largest were at the bottom and extended close to the ground, almost touching, which made the tree extremely climbable. Perhaps the most curious of all, however, was the bark of that copper beech. It was silver in color and perfectly smooth to the touch. Names and initials had been etched here and there, but the most noticeable tree-graffiti was carved into the bark at approximately eye-level. Yes, right there, looking straight into the eyes of anyone who comes across that tree, is the phrase:

'This Is My Beloved Self In Whom I Am Well-Pleased.'

"Whilst marveling, I moved backwards – the way marveling people often do – as if distance would shed some light on the meaning of this inscription. Nothing-of-the-sort occurred. After I backed away approximately fifteen feet, I tripped over something covered by orange pine needles. While still on my hands and knees, I crawled over to get a look at the cause of my tumble. I brushed away the pine needles and discovered a triangular, red and white traffic sign. Written on the sign in red block letters was this word:

'Yield.'

"It seemed like that **Yield** sign was covering an object of some kind. It only made sense that something more substantial was behind my fall. My suspicions proved to be correct. When I removed the sign, I unearthed a wheel that was attached to a door protruding from the ground. Immediately, without a second thought, I decided that it was my duty to open the portal. I've never felt so curious before in my life. I really had this burning, unquenchable desire to see what exactly laid in wait directly beneath my feet.

"It wasn't easy turning that wheel. It was old and rusty. Obviously, it hadn't been used in ages. But eventually, after what I would describe as a strong-healthy push, I managed to loosen it just enough. From that point onward, turning the wheel was quite easy, although oddly time consuming. It seemed to turn, and turn, and turn, to no end. Finally, though, the wheel twisted as far as it would go, and I lifted it – despite its considerable weight.

"What happened next, reminds me of my favorite *National Geographic* television special about cave exploration in New Mexico.

"The instant I opened the door I was greeted by a chilling, non-stop wind that billowed forth directly into my face. Along with that everlasting breath of air, came a foreboding, spine-chilling howling. I looked downward and saw an iron ladder that appeared to lead deep into the earth and disappeared into utter darkness. I remember looking down into the hole. I remember thinking the bellowing I heard may have been a product of wind speed and other miscellaneous factors. But, I also felt that it could have been some kind of demonic mating call of sorts – a call that emanated from an old friend of mine: The Abomination of Desolation. That dastardly bastard was probably down there in that abyss, waiting for a follow-up interview with yours truly.

"Just as I was about to make my way down the ladder and into that pitch-black, never-ending shaft, I heard a sweet, enchanting melody creep forth and weave its way through the pine trees surrounding me. It sounded as if members of an orchestra of elves were playing a strange, yet sacred, medieval fugue on harps and assorted musical pipes - predominantly the flageolet, a type of fipple flute. I was totally enveloped, not to mention, totally enraptured by the mesmerizing harmony that played upon the old factory senses in my ears.

"Futilely, I looked over to see from whence the music came, and that's precisely when my mind began to whirl-a-bit. Visions of gigantic, dancing sugar daddies, chuckles, and goobers invaded my head and beckoned me to sleep. Suffix it to say, I could not resist their call, and I fell into a deep slumber – right then and there.

"The next thing I knew, I found myself lying prostrate on the ground. I must have been out cold for a long time because the sun was gone and a half-moon had appeared. The pines, the beech tree, the sheep, the columns, the stone head, the door, everything – they were all gone. And when I sat up, I discovered that I was on freshly mowed grass on the edge of that spheroid forest - right by the off-ramp where I began my quest. I'm clueless as to how I returned to the spot. Most surprisingly, though, I noticed that my red emergency gas tank was only two feet from my head – and it was filled, to the nozzle, with gasoline.

"One last footnote. Upon waking from my deep-sleep and situating myself, a name and phrase continuously ricocheted throughout my head.

'Sylvanus A. Mosherbutts,' said a voice. 'Sylvanus A. Mosherbutts. He is not dead, but sleepeth. Sylvanus A. Mosherbutts. He is not dead, but sleepeth.'

Those words invaded my brain, from one side to the other. 'He is not dead, but sleepeth.'"

That was it.

Wayne seemed to believe I'd have a response that would explain everything that happened to him.

"Well?" he said, as he turned toward me. "What do you think of my story? And please, don't beat off around the bush. Be honest. Tell me if you think I just told you a ridiculous, cock and balls story."

Unfortunately, I told him just that.

"I don't mean to upset you Wayne," I said, "but you're a fucking idiot. You passed out by the off-ramp and imagined everything. You were dehydrated and slightly more delusional than usual."

"More delusional than usual?"

"Yeah," I replied, "more delusional than usual."

Of course, he then countered my logic by muttering a predictable and, for him, totally sensible question.

"Then how do you explain the fact that my emergency gas can was totally full?"

My answer was simple.

"Pretty easily," I told him. "You're such a moron, I bet you were carrying a full gas can – from the moment you left your car, until the moment you woke up on the grass. Also, I think you meant to say suffice it to say and olfactory."

Wayne looked disappointed and didn't answer. Instead, he abruptly turned away from me and made his way back to the car. Since he provided the means for me to get home, I followed.

Twenty minutes later, after an awkward and speechless ride, I found myself sitting in the driveway, about to part ways with the Patron-Saint-Of-Hare-Brained-Schemes. I moved to open the car door and leave, but Wayne put his hand on my shoulder and stopped me. Then, as he stared straight ahead, he told me I was "acting like a doubting-dumb-ass" and I needed to "adjust my attitude."

In response, and in order to make him feel better, I told him that his story "may, in fact, be partly true."

"I would have to see it to believe it," I added.

"No, no. You poor, poor, soul," he said gravely, while maintaining zero eye contact. "You've got it all backwards. You have to *believe* it to *see* it. If *you* go back there, *you* probably won't notice half the shit I saw. Maybe nothing at all. Besides, it's probably too late for you anyhow. That's okay though, I'm not going to induce-labor the point any longer."

"This isn't *The Polar Express*, Wayne."

"Yeah, well, listen for a moment," he said. "Before you go, despite the fact that you insist on pursuing your nay-saying-ways, I want to invite you to a dinner party. It's at my house next Thursday and I'm the host. My brothers and fathers have already RSVP'd. You might be the guest of honor, so I need you to be there. Hors d'oeuvres will be served promptly at 6:30, then a top secret entree, and an extra special dessert to follow."

"Oh, and one other thing," he said. "This is an odd request, but indulge me, will you? I want you to write a poem for me about **Exit Thirty-Three B**. Do you think you could do that? Just fax it to me when you're done."

I wanted to go to bed so I didn't ask any questions. I said yes to his request and told him I'd write a poem as soon as possible.

Then, I accepted his dinner invitation and closed the car door. He floored the Crown Victoria in reverse and peeled out down the street. I stood still in the driveway and waited until the sound of his engine and muffler trailed off completely. A neighbor's dog barked a couple of times, and I disappeared down the driveway.

"You know, Dr. Drinkwater, I've been thinking
a lot about it, and I've come to the conclusion
that mankind shouldn't be out in space,
really deep underwater, or riding on other
animals - especially horses. It's just weird, if
you consider the natural order of things."

-WAYNE

"You're getting there, Wayne. You're on the right
track. In the end, I guess humans just can't overcome
the desire to go exactly where they don't belong. Now,
if you don't mind, I've got some work to finish up…"

-DR. DRINKWATER

Dialogue from a rare encounter
and a brief conversation

CHAPTER 18

Exit Thirty-Three B: Inspected

THE NEXT DAY - I believe it was a Sunday - I happened to have some extra time on my hands, so I set out to inspect **Exit Thirty-Three B** for myself. I remember the day well because the weather was, once again, near perfect. The afternoon air was warm, but comfortable and dry. The sun's rays shone down as bright as ever. There wasn't a single cloud hovering above me in the sky. There was also this feeling of stillness, as if everything was closed and everyone had stayed home for the day.

When I arrived at **Exit Thirty-Three B**, I saw that Wayne was right. At first glance, that fourth, lucky leaf looked rather typical. Just like any other off-ramp-circular-woodland, the circumference of it was quite unkempt and riddled with litter and other rejected items. Also, just as Wayne related, piercing through the wild brush proved to be a tedious, painstaking task. Nevertheless, I maintained my resolve and made my way through the thorns, twigs, and poison ivy. Soon enough, I entered a strange, much-overlooked forest.

And again, for the third time in a row, Wayne's description turned out to be surprisingly accurate. I discovered that pine trees really *were* absolutely everywhere and the ground *was* completely covered with orange pine needles. As I walked upon the needles and meandered my way through those pines, part of me, perhaps one percent, felt as if something magical and out of the ordinary might occur. The remaining ninety-nine percent felt that Wayne was probably hiding behind a tree, waiting for the perfect moment to burst forth in his Stinky-Winky costume.

Anyhow, I must have been near the center of the circle when I saw something of note – along a dip in the terrain – not too far off in the distance. I made my way over posthaste and was confronted by a ramshackle, hodgepodge dwelling – a wood-land home that must have been constructed by a rare, go-get-ting-squatter. Relatively speaking, it looked like a pretty decent shack. Apart from the clear, vinyl shower curtains - used to cre-ate a pleasant, wrap-around porch - the abode would have fit perfectly in the upper-class, historical district of a 1930s shanty town. The walls of the place were made of stone and rusty cor-rugated iron served as its roof. To add character, there was also a Victorian-style turret and a red brick chimney – complete with a decorative, copper-turned-green cap.

I sized up this architectural phenomenon for a couple of min-utes and poked around its grounds. Eventually, though, I had to know whether or not the pioneering owner was home – although that appeared unlikely. I knocked several times on a round top door made out of thick pine tree branches, but no one answered my call. Then, after some semi-intense, internal deliberation, and the application of a brief cost-benefit analysis, I took a gamble and invited myself into the house. I'm not sure if laws against breaking and entering apply to the homesteads of squatters, but at the time

I believed the pros slightly outweighed the cons. Conveniently, the front door had no lock, so entry was easier than expected.

Immediately upon crossing the threshold, I realized that I had stumbled upon a true paragon of practical and prudent interior design. The mysterious lair's layout was open and airy and downright pleasing to the eye. Its rustic look and its subtle, yet methodical composition, made me feel at peace and right at home.

My self-guided tour went as follows:

The first room I entered was a living room of sorts, which boasted a pine tree-trunk coffee table and a pickup truck bench-seat – complete with pleated, gray, vinyl upholstery. I then walked into the kitchen section, which included an antique cast iron stove and the ultimate makeshift dining table. Two traffic signs served as the surface of the table – an orange "Be Prepared To Stop: Trucks Entering and Exiting the Road" and a yellow "We Love Our Children: Please Drive Carefully" – and were attached to two wooden cable reels. In what probably serves as the bedroom, there was a mattress filled with pine needles and some blankets placed on top of a collection of plastic milk crates. Beside the bed, was a nightstand made from a red, plastic bucket that said "Bio-hazard." On top of the bio-hazard bucket was a half-eaten breakfast burrito, the remnants of several deviled eggs, and some luxury hand lotion made from Japanese seaweed extract.

The bedroom also had some nice bookcases, which were built with concrete blocks, as well as sand-filled bottles and cans. For a decrepit shack in the woods, the library had a fairly extensive multimedia collection and contained such gems as a Rod Stewart eight-track tape (featuring *Do Ya Think I'm Sexy?*), a VHS movie called *Nightdreams*, and an incomplete set of the *Encyclopedia Britannica*. My favorite finds, however, were two books by an author named Wilhelm Fauhknerz titled *The Soft and the Furry* and *As I Die, Lying*. Another book caught my eye by an author named O. Billingtons. It was titled *Squatters Rights for the Average Squatter: A Case Law Compendium*.

After approximately ten minutes, my snooping was complete, so I went outside and positioned myself on a moss-covered tree stump. I sat there and waited a fair amount of time, maybe fifteen minutes or so, but to no avail. The owner never came home.

Alas, dusk was settling in, so I decided to wrap up my off-ramp adventure and call it a day.

Sadly, I didn't experience leprechaun music, portals leading to hell, or any sheep climbing up trees. All I discovered was a shack, occupied by a reclusive polymath-squatter. The guy probably whacks-off nightly with his luxurious, top-of-the-line hand lotion.

"Who's the cat's father? Now, that's what I want to know. Too many stray female felines out there, gallivanting in alleys, going at it buck-wild. Why? Well, it's because they lack a strong father figure, and I've had about enough of it."

-WAYNE

During a moment of high tension, discussing the factors behind the surplus cat population

CHAPTER 19

There's No Place Like Home?

———

NIGHT HAD FALLEN BY THE time I made it back to the pool. I was more tired than usual, so I didn't take a moment to stand in the darkness and listen to the pump, the heater, or any other miscellaneous pool-side sounds. Instead, I promptly crammed myself between the bushes and the fence and flipped the light switch.

When I emerged from the bushes, I saw a sight for sore eyes: a shining light emanating from the deep end, bright blue water, and the magnificent, yellow HMS Talbot. The friendly Talbot was by itself, waiting patiently for me in the shallow end. Without a thought, I grabbed the skimmer attached to an aluminum pole and dragged my vessel toward the stairs.

Per usual, entry was difficult, but, once again, I climbed aboard flawlessly. Not a single drop of water made contact with my suit. Then, I properly arranged myself after a brief, but worthwhile struggle. I comfortably positioned my head on the bow and dangled my feet over the stern, just above the water.

CHAPTER 20

Three of Three:
Point, Counter-Point

———

IT'S THE DEAD OF NIGHT and there I am - standing alone atop a cliff, looking out upon the cold black sky. Everything is still and quiet - until - about a mile below me, a locomotive appears. My eyes zero in on it and I watch as it drags a row of cars tooth and nail through the desert. I study its movement and I can sense that something is unbalanced and askew. The locomotive moves too fast. It struggles to hold and desperately clings to the tracks. The whistle blares and steam escapes. Black smoke spews from its stack. Its massive wheels turn and turn and its pistons pump. Each rod shifts furiously back and forth. Here and there, embers flitter through the air, and vanish in the iron wyvern's wake.

In a flash, I find myself aboard the train. I've joined two angry men who await delivery in the dining car. One is middle-aged, the other is older and bloated. The well-dressed pair look similar - most likely father and son. They share sharp, cutting eyes, and red-hot-hairless-heads. They sit at either end of a lengthy mahogany table, silverware ready and waiting in front of them: forks to the left, knives to the right, empty plates in the middle. I sit between the silent men at the center of the table, my presence unacknowledged. I watch them as they stare fixedly at one another, their blood boiling as it travels through their veins. The stillness of the scene is difficult to bear, and is magnified by a low hiss that slowly creeps into the room.

A burst of noise. One of the two doors slides open and quickly closes. A butler has entered the dining car. He carries with him two silver platters, one in each hand. He sets the first dish in front of the son and lifts the lid. A trail of steam is released along with a metallic clang. He nods to the son and carefully makes his way past me to the other side. The father removes a large handkerchief from his suitcoat and stuffs it into his collar. The white cloth flows out from his neck and covers his torso. The butler serves him and nods. He slides the door open, slides the door shut, and he's gone without a word.

The ill-tempered pair commence dining and a vicious argument erupts within seconds. I listen intently, but I can't decipher the words that flow back and forth from their angry mouths. The frantic, chugging train overpowers the dispute and the hiss steadily increases in volume. The old man can't hear what his son says. The son can't hear what the old man says. They repeat themselves, but the cycle can't be stopped. Outside the car, the locomotive's wheels feverishly turn and turn and the pistons pump. The water level is too low. The pressure is too high. The boiler barrel is about to blow.

The father reaches the end of his tether. Intense and filled with passion, he grasps his meat pierced fork and slams his clenched fist onto the table. He aims the pointer finger of his free hand directly at his counterpart and unloads - his jaws violently open and close repeatedly. His son retaliates without missing a beat. He jumps to his feet, his chair falls behind him, and he aims his pointer finger - savagely - at his father's heart. He issues a counterpoint neither of us saw coming. The old man motions for water, but it's too late. His hands clutch his throat and immediately move to his chest. He slouches and falls to the floor.

The son sprints across the car. He places his hands on his father's abdomen and thrusts downward. But the old man can't regurgitate. He can only writhe, wriggle, and squirm on the floor. The son switches tactics and thrusts downward on his father's chest over and over again. But it's too late. The old man's lips are blue and he loses consciousness. Darkness drops over his eyes.

Precisely at that moment, I sense a presence behind me. I turn and gaze out the dining car's window and see that a committee of vultures has formed above us. The desert birds hiss and circle longingly - ready and waiting - in the dark-red-sky. Ahead, a blood dimmed disc patiently emerges from the horizon. Its crimson glow gradually grows and stretches farther and farther into the night. The train, however, inches dutifully toward its destination. Its stack disgorges black smoke - puff after puff after puff.

"Your mother is right, Barry. 'Don't speak ill of the dead.' Just think ill of them."

- DR. DRINKWATER.

CHAPTER 21

Gary-Spelled-Like-Gerry: Another Rendezvous

———

I'M NOT SURE WHAT EXACTLY woke me up. It may have been any number of things: a pebble or two thrown in the pool, something or other rustling in the trees, or simply my name whispered repeatedly.

What I do know, however, is that I wasn't ready to transition from sleep world to every-day existence. As a result, I was in a state of panic, sweating profusely, and unaware of my surroundings. Luckily, though, my fit of terror was only temporary. After a brief moment of self-reflection, I figured out who I was, where I was, and what I was doing.

When I fully regained control of my faculties, I decided it would be best to make my way ashore to solid ground. I don't think I was asleep for long, but, then again, I was unaware of the time. Regardless, it dawned on me that I probably should have retreated to my bedroom when I returned home - not a raft in the pool. I knew this interruption in my sleep greatly diminished my chances of returning to slumber.

I managed to disembark from the Talbot in only a minute or two. I almost reached the pool-house when a miniature voice crept up from behind me.

"Ba-barry? Ba-ba-barry?" the voice said. "Hello? Ba-barry?"

I wasn't startled. I knew Gary-Spelled-Like-Gerry was trailing me - probably at a distance that maximized proximity while preserving the ability to flee.

"Yes, Gary-Spelled-Like-Gerry," I answered. "It's me. How are you tonight?"

I turned around nonchalantly and looked at him. I could see the little guy, but only the outline of his frame - I had flipped the light switch after I returned to land.

He didn't respond.

I suppose he was a bit bewildered by the fact that I asked him a question about his well-being.

"What's going on, Gary-Spelled-Like-Gerry?" I repeated. "How are you? What can I do for you?"

Still perplexed and distrustful, he slowly put together a question for me.

"I...I...I...was just wah-wah-wondering something. My fa-fa-friend at school, Ja-Ja-Johnny Levinson, says that bah-bah-blood is ba-ba-blue when it's in-sa-side of you. Is that ta-ta-true?"

Gary-Spelled-Like-Gerry stepped back a foot.

"Do you mean inside of me specifically," I said, "or do you mean inside all human beings?"

"Ba-ba-both, Barry. Unless your ba-ba-blood is different than other pee-pull's ba-blood. I guess I ja-ja-just don't want my blood to be bah-ba-blue."

"Well, my blood is the same as anyone's blood - and it's red. Blood is red as it flows through the human body. Usually a dark red. I'm glad you're thinking more critically than usual."

Gary-Spelled-Like-Gerry didn't appear satisfied. In fact, he looked disappointed. He stood there with his head down and his hands clasped behind his back - his signature pose. Once again, he said nothing.

"What, Gary-Spelled-Like-Gerry? What's the problem?"

His head angled upward slightly and it seemed as though he was looking me in the eyes.

"Wah-well," he pleaded, "Jah-Johnny Levinson sah-says the only reason blood la-la-looks red is because it ga-goes from bah-blue to red when it rah-ra-reaches the air. He says that's when it ox-ox-uh-dies-ehz. Ox-ox-oh-uh-da-day-shun."

I thought Gary-Spelled-like-Gerry would back up another foot or two after he said that nonsense. He surprised me, though, and kept his ground when I answered him.

"Johnny Levinson is a fucking moron," I explained, "and I bet his parents are morons too. I don't know why they told him something as stupid as that."

My brother had a response at the ready.

"His fa-father, is a fa-fa-leb-o-tah-tom-ah-ist," he said. "And tha-tha bah-blood in my aah-ah-arm looks grah-green-ish-ba-blue."

"I don't know what to tell you, pal, but I think you've been looking at your greenish-blue veins too much. I recommend you find yourself a flashlight, go to your room, turn off the lights, stick yourself in the closet, and close the door. While in there, take your flashlight and shine the light underneath your wrist. Then, you'll probably realize your blood is red as it flows through your veins."

Again, Gary-Spelled-Like-Gerry spoke up right away. Perhaps he was starting to feel too comfortable with me.

"I...I...I...don't want to go into a da-dark closet," he protested. "That's tear-tear-uh-fi-ing."

"Not many people want to spend time in dark closets, Gary-Spelled-Like-Gerry, but sometimes you have to do something you don't want to do. That's how you learn. Do you know what I mean?"

He looked disheartened yet again, so I brought up the elephant in the air.

"I'm not going to chase after you this time."

He said nothing and stared at the ground.

"Just go inside," I suggested, "and take my advice. You'll be happy you did - especially after you make your great discovery."

Gary-Spelled-Like-Gerry didn't make a peep. He just turned around and walked casually toward the gate at the other side of the pool. When he was within ten feet of it, however, he converted to lightning speed and hurtled through the opening in an instant.

And then he was gone.

After my conversation with him, I continued to the pool-house - so I could finally catch some sleep. When I arrived at the door, I saw an orange poster taped to it. It contained the following words:

NOTICE TO QUIT

Dearest Barry,

Alas, the zero hour approaches. The countdown has begun. Soon, you must part ways with the pool-house.

As you can surely understand, it is time for you to find a real job and a suitable place to call your own.

A man does not become a man by remaining a pool-boy forever. You have persisted as a *porcellum lactantem* for too long and must be weaned from your life of leisure.

Believe me, this is as difficult for us as it is for you (perhaps even more so for us).

A new tenant is due to move in on the first of January, also known as New Year's Day.

We have invested in a pool-cleaning robot.

Please be advised:

If you have not vacated the pool-house by December the twenty-fourth, a sheriff will be on hand to serve you with a *Summary Process Summons and Complaint.*

In other words, **Hereof Fail Not**, or the due course of law shall be utilized to evict you from the premises.

We know you will do the right thing.

For more information concerning the eviction process, please refer to Massachusetts General Laws: Chapter 186, Section 12.

Your Mother,
Priscilla Drinkwater

I knew this eviction notice was coming for me. It was just a matter of time. I grabbed it from the door, folded it into a small square, and stuck it in my pocket. Then, I proceeded inside and climbed into bed. Somehow, it didn't take long for me to succumb to sleep - even with Barrie across the room, looking at me, angrily, with his hateful, piercing eyes.

"It's tough to go a-fishing these days - especially when some vile snake crept out in the middle of the night and stocked every pond with red herring."

-WAYNE

CHAPTER 22A

The Mirro Building

———◆———

I PASSED THROUGH A REVOLVING door and entered the lobby of
the Mirro Building at least ten minutes before my noon appointment. I headed toward the reception desk and was immediately
confronted with an industrial-sized photograph of the Mirro
Building and its surroundings. The glossy, framed, black and
white photo was fixed to the wall behind the counter and loomed
imposingly over the foyer. It must have been a good seven feet in
height and ten feet in width.

In the photograph, the Mirro Building looked a wee-bit different to me than it does when I'm traveling on the highway at
sixty-five miles an hour. I suppose it appeared more impressive
and commanding - perhaps because it had been cropped and iso-
lated in the composition. I'm not really sure. Nonetheless, the
seven-story building seemed both in and out of place. On the one
hand, the modern structure's sleek, shiny glass and box-like shape
looked distinctly synthetic - perfectly unnatural. On the other
hand, the office building seemed to fit within its pastoral setting -
thanks, most likely, to the glass, which reflected a placid river,
evergreen trees, and the hill on which it stood.

I didn't want to be late for my interview, so I ceased my analysis of the photo and abruptly took off toward a directory. I thought I'd find suite 307 easily and on my own, but I encountered a great deal of trouble when I tried to locate it. For whatever reason, it was nowhere to be found on the third floor. I could see rooms 300-306 and rooms 308 to 310, but 307 was suspiciously absent. After several aggravating minutes, though, my eyes finally fell upon the number 307. According to the map, it was situated - inexplicably - between rooms 605 and 609 on the sixth floor.

My 12:00 appointment was minutes away, so I left the foyer and made my way toward some elevators at the end of the hall. As I left the lobby, however, I heard a voice call for my attention.

"Excuse me, sir," the voice said. "Can I help you, sir?"

I could tell by the tone the person wasn't truly interested in helping me. The formal words were polite enough, but I knew better. Besides, my time of need had come and gone, so I pretended I didn't hear the question and continued down the hallway. Futilely, the voice persisted until I could hear it no more.

"Young man, young man" the voice continued. "Can I help you with something? Sir..."

When I got to the end of the hall, I realized I must have seen a mirage: There were no elevators - only a turn in the hallway that led to another one. It didn't take long - after a couple lefts here and rights there - to lose myself deep within the bowels of the Mirro Building. One would think - with a glass exterior and all - that natural light would be near and abundant, but that simply wasn't the case. The interior was gloomy - lit by ineffective fluorescent lights in the ceiling - and labyrinthine - comprised of offices, never-ending corridors, artificial plant life and sterile, non-offensive art.

Eventually, after I took one of many lefts, I came upon a break in the pattern. Before me, I saw yet another hallway, but an abnormally long one, darker and without any doorways on either side. I stood at the beginning of it and contemplated my next move. I knew I was late, or was going to be late. However, I wasn't sure if I should turn around and cut my losses, or continue down the hall. It was a difficult decision and I would have turned back - if I hadn't seen what looked like a person appear, and hastily disappear, at the end of the hall.

The last time I encountered another human being was in the main lobby, so I figured I'd take a gamble and see just what I would encounter at the end of the hall. At first, all I could hear was the sound of my own footsteps. When I neared the end of the hall, though, I could hear grunting, some foul language, and what sounded like someone striking an inanimate object.

My ears didn't deceive me. When I turned the corner to see the commotion, I witnessed a curious crime in progress. There, in an Art Deco-like sub-lobby - with a checkered tile floor and two elevators on either side - I saw a distinguished looking old man whacking a vending machine with his umbrella. He wore a derby hat, a black trench coat, matching pants, and black Oxford dress shoes. He also sported a chevron mustache, a devilish ducktail beard, and pince-nez eyeglasses. A combination lock briefcase stood next to him at his feet.

The man didn't see me, which gave me a moment to assess the peculiar situation. Counterintuitively, I decided that he was approachable and he would know where to direct me - despite the unsettling vending machine violence. I waited until he landed another substantial blow upon the machine, and, from a safe distance, made my move.

"Excuse me, sir," I said. "Pardon my interruption, but I'm looking for room 307. Could you tell me where it is?"

The man wasn't the least bit startled. He slowly swiveled toward me, looked me up and down, and return-swiveled to face the vending machine. He replied with his back to me.

"It's the old bait and switch," he remarked disdainfully. "You pay for top-notch, you see, and you get nothing - or a cheap impostor."

He walloped the 8050 Hot Beverage Merchandiser with his umbrella once more and it came to life. I heard some grinding and then some hot liquid - a buff-brown color - trickled into a cup. He picked it up and inspected it thoroughly - his eyes hovered just above the brim.

"Well," he added, "the victory goes to that ever-present, colorless, odorless gas, commonly known as the man. But, at least I got the better hand."

He turned and presented his red, black, and white playing card cup to me.

The mouth under the mustache continued to move.

"They call this a royal flush," he said. "An ace, a king, a queen, a jack, and a ten - all in the same suit, all diamonds. Too bad my whipped, gourmet, French vanilla coffee - with sugar and whitener - looks a bit weak and peaked, eh?"

"That's true," I replied. "It looks like you've been flim-flammed, but at least you showed that machine who's boss. Still, it's hard to believe a robot like that would produce a deluxe beverage."

The man furrowed his brow, half offended and half amused.

"Hmmm...I see," he said. "So you say you're looking for room 307, eh?"

"Yes, I am - but I've lost my bearings, if you know what I mean."

"Young man, I hate to tell you this, but it isn't easy getting to 307," he informed me. "You'll have to put a little pep in your step, a little oomph in your poomph."

"Oomph in my what?" I asked.

"Yes, you heard correctly. So, now, let me level with you. Generally speaking, you have to go up to go down, across to go around."

"How about specifically speaking?"

"Okay, okay, settle down," he said. "Specifically speaking, my advice to you is to get in one of these elevators here, head up to the seventh floor, take two lefts, and walk straight until you get to another set of elevators. Go down one floor, take a right, and follow that corridor until you reach a water bubbler and a rubber weeping fig tree. The door across from the bubbler and the fig should be room 307. Now, if you'll excuse me. I'm off to pierce the corporate veil."

With that, the man turned and picked up his briefcase. He faced me once again and bowed ever so slightly.

"Bon voyage," he said, rapidly. "Perhaps we'll meet again. Until then."

I thanked him for the directions and watched him as he took off down the hallway with his coffee in hand. I pushed the button to beckon the elevator and waited for it to arrive.

The Coffee Table

———

I KNEW IT HAD TO be beyond 12:00, so I took the eccentric man's advice. I definitely doubted his round-a-bout directions, but there was no time for dawdling. I felt better, however, once the second elevator opened to the sixth floor. After I took a right and walked down the hallway, all became even more promising. The rubber weeping fig tree, the water bubbler, and door 307 were all there, just as he foretold.

Despite my tardiness, I knew there was a chance my interview dreams could still come true. So, I put on my pleasant disposition costume, opened the door, and stepped into the office suite. The first thing I saw was a school-house-looking clock, which read 12:15, and then a receptionist, sitting at a desk on the other side of a glass partition. He paid no attention to me whatsoever, even though I could tell he knew I was there. The guy was looking down and reading, pretending to look busy.

I decided a gentle, two-fingered, knuckle-knock to the glass would be the best way to get a response. Fortunately, it did the trick. He rolled his eyes upward without moving his head - in irritation and disapproval - and slid the glass window to one side. He didn't say anything, stared at me, and waited for me to fill the verbal void.

"Hello," I said. "My name is Barry Drinkwater. I'm here for my 12:00 appointment, but I'm a little late."

He sighed and responded robotically and reluctantly.

"Courtroom Abstract Artist?" he inquired.

"Yes."

"The next applicant will be late as well. Your interview will be with Ms. Viola Rollins. It will begin at 12:30 and should end at 1:15. You may take a seat."

He raised his hand to the glass once again and slid it shut. I turned to find a seat in the waiting room and saw that I was the only person in the poorly lit space. I found a plush chair in the corner, next to an end table with a lamp on it. Then, because I truly enjoy waiting room reading material, I leaned toward the coffee table in front of me and waded through my options.

There were several gossip magazines spread out on the coffee table, a book of Norman Rockwell paintings, and Grandma Moses' autobiography. Although any of those offerings would have satisfied me, I was most interested in two books, which were stashed under the pile. The first was titled *Bidet! The True, Uncensored, and Previously Untold Story of Biddelay Babergé: The Inventor of the World's Finest Bath Accoutrement,* and the second was titled *The Fifty Greatest Men in American History.*

It was difficult to choose one over the other, but, in the end, I couldn't resist a macho-virile collection of American heroes. The book's gold leaf border, and Hieronymus Bosch-esque illustration of a fox hunt in progress, were just too enigmatic and enticing to ignore. The scene on the cover, titled *Fox Hunt in the Garden of Nature's Travails*, prominently featured Teddy Roosevelt and Andrew Jackson, center left. Accompanied by a pack of foxhounds, they rode tandem on an elegant horse as they dashed over a small stream and brandished their rifles, tally-ho.

Cornelius Vanderbilt, Andrew Carnegie, and Thomas Edison also rode atop horses, which galloped furiously after Roosevelt and Jackson in hot pursuit. On the bottom left corner of the painting, a large hound lunged at a fox that carried a miniature Ronald Reagan in its mouth. The fox was running at full speed and its pointy teeth were clasped around Reagan's neck. The furry red prey was captured in mid-air, as if it was preparing to jump off the cover of the book. In the distant background, I spotted Patrick Henry, Robert E. Lee, and Herbert Hoover. The three of them were loitering by a stone farm wall - most likely discussing the trials and triumphs of the hunt.

I opened the book, casually flipped through its pages, and found that a short biography was devoted to each great and venerable man. Coupled with these profiles were pen and ink drawings that deified the heroes and featured them in various states of glory. On one page, Paul Revere rode off into the moonlight on his horse, chased and shot at by the King's men. On another page, George Washington stood in a small boat as he crossed the Delaware. Sharks circled the craft and their heads peeked out above the surface. I could see their black beady eyes, wide open mouths, and sharp, terrible teeth.

My favorite biography, however, was number thirty-three - Rumpelstiltskin's. The biography and illustration were positioned matter-of-factly between Walt Disney and J. Edgar Hoover. The pen and ink drawing caught my attention first, as the rendition of Rumpelstiltskin was fanciful and bewitching. He stood in the middle of a dark and densely wooded forest with one foot on the ground, the other raised slightly in the air. His profile was outlined with a bright light, which give him a spectral look. It appeared as though he was poised to perform a secret miracle.

At this point, I got up and accosted the man behind the glass once more. Annoyed, he slid the glass to one side.

"What may I help you with now, sir?" he demanded. "Your interview is in a couple of minutes."

"I was just flipping through this book," I said. "It's called *The Fifty Greatest Men in American History*, and somehow, Rumpelstiltskin is listed as one of them."

"Yes, of course," he replied coldly. "Everyone knows Rumpelstiltskin helped to secure the Northwest Territory. He was a hero at the Battle of Fallen Timbers in 1794."

Even though I knew that was crazy talk, I still felt ten percent ashamed.

"I see," I said.

The man promptly slid the glass window back into place.

Since that conversation went nowhere, I retreated to my chair in the corner. The book would have to fill in the remaining gaps.

According to the text, former Revolutionary War General, Mad Anthony Wayne, somehow summoned Rumpelstiltskin in the summer of 1794. Wayne was hell-bent at defeating the evil Indian, Blue Jacket, in order to gain possession of the Northwest

Territory. Rumpelstiltskin - heavily involved in the area's fur trade at the time - was known for his knowledge of the land and battlefield wizardry. Mad Anthony Wayne managed to persuade Rumpelstiltskin to help, and together they devised a devious scheme to defeat Blue Jacket and his men.

Three days before the battle, Rumpelstiltskin traveled deep within the forest. He danced from tree to tree with an axe and cut many of them, nearly to the point of collapsing. When he completed this task, he stood in the middle of his chopping toils to admire his handiwork. A devilish grin developed on his face and his sinister voice filled the forest:

"Timber!" he screeched.

He then leapt into the air, and with a mighty thunder, plunged his right foot straight into the ground. The trees around him fell simultaneously and he vanished in a cloud of smoke.

The day before the Battle of Fallen Timbers, Mad Anthony Wayne and his men hid amongst the fallen trees and waited for their enemies to arrive. Blue Jacket's warriors eventually appeared and foolishly thought the collapsed trunks and branches would work to their advantage. Perhaps they would hinder the advance of American forces. But they were wrong. Blue Jacket and his men were caught by surprise, outflanked, and quickly routed.

Mad Anthony Wayne was victorious.

To this day, it is unknown just what Rumpelstiltskin received in return for his assistance.

Alas, shortly after I finished reading the story of Rumpelstiltskin, my train of thought was interrupted by the receptionist.

The impatient man raised his hand, arched his eyebrows, and mouthed my name.

"Mr. Drinkwater, Mr. Drinkwater," he said when I reached the glass partition. "It's 12:30. Time for your appointment. Head right in there."

I nodded my head in agreement and placed my hand on the door-knob.

"Just go through that door right there, Mr. Drinkwater," the receptionist nudged me again. "Ms. Viola Rollins is ready for you now."

The Interview

———◆———

I OPENED THE DOOR, CROSSED the threshold, and entered a small, windowless room. Viola Rollins stood up from behind her desk.

"Hello, I'm Viola Rollins," she said. "Pleased to meet you."

She extended her arm over the desk, a wave of strongly scented floral perfume hit me, and we shook hands. Her grip was tight and she pulled me toward her. She also looked me up and down at least three times.

I introduced myself in the midst of shaking.

"I'm Barry Drinkwater," I replied. "Nice to meet you."

My voice warbled and I sounded like I was out of breath.

She gave me the up-down a couple more times and slid into a high-back, leather executive chair. I took a seat in one of those modern-looking Danish armchairs - taupe in color - which probably was better suited for a child.

The moment before the interview began was less than graceful. Sure, it lasted only seconds, but mentally and emotionally speaking, it went on for an eternity, maybe two. I admit, though, I'm partially to blame for the distressing pleasantries-to-business interlude. The thing is, while Viola surveyed me, I couldn't help but focus on certain elements of her outfit. I tried to hide it, but my eyes were drawn to her head and the beige scarf wrapped around it, tied at her neck, toothache-style. That scarf, along with her thick-rimmed amber glasses and gold clam shell necklace, made her look like she just returned from driving a convertible in the late 1950s.

Anyhow, as I tried to figure out what her ensemble - and the photo of a pointing Margaret Thatcher on the wall - indicated about her personality, Viola piped up and asked me my first question.

"Do you know where I just was?" she said, while she stared at my forehead.

I shrugged my shoulders.

"I mean it. Do *you* know where I just was?" she repeated forcefully.

"I'm sorry, but I don't know where you were."

"Well, why don't you, for the sake of your interview, take a guess."

She seemed committed to retrieving an answer from me, so I did my best to come up with something reasonable to say.

"Were you at lunch?" I guessed.

"Good job. That's correct. I was at lunch. Do you want to know what happened to me at lunch?"

"You ate some food and drank a beverage."

"Good job again!" she said. "But let me tell you something. I wanted a sandwich, but not a whole sandwich. So, I asked for a half sandwich. Do you know what the imbecile behind the counter said to me?"

I shrugged my shoulders.

"No, really," she said. "Tell me if you know what he said."

"I'm sorry, but I don't know what he said to you."

"Excuse me? Speak up."

"I said I'm sorry, but I don't know what he said."

"The young man at the counter said, 'I can't do that for you, mam. What would I do with the other half?' What do you make of that?"

"That's terrible. What kind of sandwich did you order? Was it a club sandwich?"

"What sandwich?" she asked incredulously. "Why does that matter?"

"I guess it doesn't."

"The point is...the youth in this country are woefully inept."

"Well, did you tell him he only had to use one slice of bread?" I asked.

"I'm not at a restaurant to tell the employee how to make sandwiches," she replied indignantly. "I'm at a restaurant to eat sandwiches."

"I'm sorry."

"Why are you so sorry?"

"You didn't get your half sandwich. That upsets me. I also don't know what else to say."

"Tell me this," she demanded. "What thoughts cross your mind when someone says the phrase 'life isn't fair' to you?"

"That's a really good question. Thanks for ask..."

She interrupted me right away.

"Don't placate me," she said. "Just answer the question."

"I think it's ridiculous," I explained. "Life is and isn't fair. That person probably needs to come up with a better justification for…"

She interrupted me again and stared at my forehead.

"Okay, okay," she went on, "tell me the names of four of your friends."

"I'm not sure if that's necessary."

"I want to know your friends' names and I want to know how they would describe you."

"I don't doubt that," I remarked, "but I think it would be best if we transitioned to another question."

"Very interesting! What do you think *that* says about you?"

"I'm sure my response could be interpreted in a variety of ways."

Viola Rollins looked at my forehead skeptically and fished around on her desk for my résumé. She found it under a pile of papers and quickly examined it.

"It says here on your résumé that you worked for Wang Laboratories," she noted. "Do you want to comment on that?"

"Those were some of the best days of my life."

"Would you say the world was your oyster?" she inquired impatiently.

"I'm not sure if I would use that expression."

"Could I call Wang for a reference?"

"Absolutely…"

"You're mumbling. I can't hear you."

"I said absolutely - I'm proud of the work I did there."

"I'm going to call immediately following this interview," she disclosed.

She then wrote something or other on my résumé.

"Next question: Do you know why you're here today?"

"I'm seeking employment and I'm interested - to say the least - in the Courtroom Abstract Artist position."

"That's right," she stated. "You're here because you want to be a Courtroom Abstract Artist. So let's get to the nitty gritty, shall we?"

"Okay."

She leaned in a bit and looked at me as if she wanted to have a heart to heart bonding experience. I felt uncomfortable instantly.

"Let me ask you something," she said. "Were you trained as a representational painter first? All of our Courtroom Abstract Artists need experience as realists."

"Yes," I replied. "I began as a child who drew nonsensically. I then transitioned into an artist committed to capturing the world as it is. At a certain point, though, I realized I wasn't going to progress as a representational painter. My perception of the world, and the world as it is, got closer and closer - met halfway repeatedly - but in the end, never quite aligned."

"Now, that sure was a long answer," she said. "I was wondering if you'd ever stop yapping, yapping, yapping. Anyway, even though I can't remember much of what you just said, I assume that's why you became an abstract artist. Is that correct?"

"I saw no alternative."

"Why do you think Courtroom Abstract Artists are needed?" she asked.

"They probably aren't," I told her. "But, if I had to rationalize such a job, I'd say only astute Courtroom Abstract Artists can truly convey the complexities and emotions found in America's courtrooms."

"Well now, that sure sounds interesting. I bet you prepared that response in advance. Seemed scripted."

Viola ruffled through the papers on her desk again. In the process, she knocked her pen - a gold Parker fountain pen - onto the floor. It landed on the side of her desk, equidistant from the two of us. Immediately, we found ourselves locked into a pen duel - a real battle of the wills.

Total silence.

Viola looked at my forehead. I looked at her. She looked at the pen. I looked at the pen. She looked at my forehead.

"What?" she blurted out. "Do you think we have office boys for that?"

"Office boys?" I repeated. "I didn't think there was such a thing."

"Well, we don't have them. So why don't you be a gentleman and pick up that pen for me."

"Sure, by all means," I said and conceded.

I picked up her pen and handed it to her.

"What about your portfolio?" she asked, as I returned to my particularly small chair. "Did you bring your portfolio with you?"

"No, I..."

"You what? I can't hear you."

"No, I didn't."

"You mean to say you didn't bring a portfolio?"

"Yes, that's what I mean to say."

"Why wouldn't you bring a portfolio to a Courtroom Abstract Artist interview?" she asked.

"I didn't know what to expect," I said. "Besides, a portfolio would only show you what I've accomplished, not what I..."

"Sure, sure. That's about enough. I think it's time we proceed to the CATNAP."

"The CATNAP?" I inquired politely.

"Yes, that's what I said - the CATNAP."

"What is the CATNAP?"

"The CATNAP, if you must know, is a test we use to assess prospective employees. The examination measures character and intelligence. It helps us determine which candidates will succeed here at Mirro Enterprises and which won't. Everyone takes it. Standard practice."

Viola slid open the pencil drawer of her desk and took out a packet. I could see that it said CATNAP in big letters on the cover page. There were words in smaller font beneath the CATNAP acronym, but I couldn't read them. I think I saw a small C for copyright above the P in CATNAP.

She placed the packet on her desk and began to read from it. She spoke in a loud, monotone voice. I suppose directions seem more official and serious when read that way.

"I am about to administer the CATNAP," she said, "which was developed to assess character and intelligence. When the CATNAP is complete, we will know more about you, your promise in life, and if you'll be a good fit here at Mirro Enterprises. The CATNAP is divided into at least three sections. Your performance will determine how many sections you are subjected to, as well as the length of the testing period."

After that introduction and a couple more equally boring words, Viola began to administer the CATNAP. I don't want to get bogged down in all of the details, but the test was undoubtedly unorthodox. For example, one section was entirely devoted to pronunciation. Viola pointed at words such as tiramisu, mayonnaise, and applicable and then asked me to say them aloud. Other sections involved questions about office parks and condoms, eating soup in the rain, and provocatively dressed mannequins. Toward the end of the bizarre audit-of-sorts, I had to answer a convoluted question about pets and their names.

Anyhow, the interview came to a close as soon as I finished answering a hypothetical essay question. It had something to do with falling asleep in a closet during an open house. Viola abruptly closed the CATNAP booklet, told me my time was up, and motioned for me to leave. I looked up at that clock and saw that it was already 1:15. Apparently, time passes quickly when a person is subjected to an aberrant examination. She turned to me and analyzed my forehead one last time.

"It was a pleasure to meet you, Mr. Drinkwater," she said.

I told her the feeling was mutual.

I thought that was going to be it, but just before I left her office she had more to say.

"As I'm sure you realize," she stated, "we received a multitude of applications for the Courtroom Abstract Artist vacancy. And, thus far, we've been pleasantly surprised by the number of dynamic, well-qualified candidates. However, things are what they are, and we only have one vacuum to fill. So ultimately, at the end of the day, when all is said and done, what we need is an artist who values our mission - an artist who lives and breathes all things Mirro Enterprises."

"Thank you for this opportunity, Ms. Rollins," I said just as I put my hand on the doorknob. "I will never forget this interview."

With that, I softly opened and closed her office door and walked by the receptionist stationed behind the sliding glass. I considered saying goodbye in some way, but I could tell his indifference toward me was stronger than ever. Instead, I decided to take a second look at *Bidet!* and the *The Fifty Greatest Men in American History.* After all, the waiting room was empty, so I felt free to act suspiciously. As luck would have it, though, both were missing from the coffee table. Sure, I could have inquired about them, but I knew I'd be stonewalled if I asked about their whereabouts. Besides, I didn't want to push my luck too much.

Truth is, I didn't want anyone to catch me with the CATNAP tucked under my jacket. Miraculously, I was able to abscond with it from Viola's office, completely undetected. I took it right from under her nose.

"When a machine replaced me as a tollbooth collector, I knew the state of Massachusetts made a big mistake. How could a machine, *a machine*, perform the same tasks as a human being? I'm a well-trained, professional tollbooth collector! You've got to be kidding me! But the commuters will miss me. Yep, they'll revolt and stand up for me. They'll bring this injustice straight to the statehouse. I know they'll call me back to work eventually. I haven't heard yet, but I will soon. Mark my words."

-WAYNE

CHAPTER 23

The Elision
Or
Dinner Party with the Donner Party:
A Case of Civil Incivility

———

As CLEARLY INSTRUCTED, I ARRIVED at the House of Wayne, also known as Spit-House, promptly at 6:30 p.m. At the exact moment I pressed down on the bell, Stefan opened the front door armed with some unexpected etiquette and enthusiasm. It was quite something to be confronted by such a wide, courteous smile, twinkling eyes, and an equally perplexing, yet complimentary greeting.

"Ah, my dear Mr. Drinkwater," said Stefan. "How kind of you to join us tonight! Daresay, I must admit you look particularly ravishing in that suit of yours. And such a pleasant countenance, indeed! I suppose that's why you're my favorite of all Wayne's friends. Do come inside, sir. We have a special place already set for you at the dinner table."

The next thing I knew, Stefan announced my arrival to the rest of his formally attired family. I was standing in the dining room doorway when he introduced me to them.

"I now present to you, my good fellows," he proclaimed, "our guest of honor tonight – one Mr. Barry Drinkwater, son of Dr. and Mrs. Drinkwater."

And with that, the entire quintuplet gang, their fathers, Gary and Nick, as well as Choppinwood, simultaneously curtsied to me.

Immediately following this uncomfortable and bizarre mass curtsey, I noticed that Wayne wasn't present at the dinner table. Just as I opened my mouth to inquire as to his whereabouts, Stefan interjected once more.

"I will now open an envelope," he said, "that Wayne, our kind and generous brother, left for us."

Stefan retrieved a pink envelope from his inner suit coat pocket. Then, he opened it with a brass letter opener that some-one conveniently placed – next to a small golden bell – on the dinner table.

Inside the envelope was a letter from Wayne, which Stefan proceeded to read to all of us. He used a high-pitched accent, reminiscent of the Queen of England's voice.

"First and foremost," he said, "the good news is that all of you are together and within arm's length of each other tonight. All too often we forget how lucky we are to have one another. Pigeons would be much more valued by society if only there were less of them. I've often been told that a bird buried in the sand is worth at least two dollars and fifty cents hidden in a bush. So please, let me thank you for taking time out of your busy sched-ules to attend my dinner. Also, let me humbly request that you now join hands - yes, even you, Choppinwood - with the persons sitting next to you, as Stefan reads what remains of this letter.

"Now, for the bad news. Due to circumstances beyond my control - and the interior decorating motives of others - I will not be able to join you fine gentlemen as you dine this evening. Please understand that I am more than chop-fallen, but, at the same time, less than or equal to the opposite of devastatingly upset. However, as you can surely see, a place has been set for me at the table. It is my belief that despite the absence of my physical being, my spirit will still be there, sitting amongst those I hold dearest to my heart. If you don't mind, I would like you to serve my empty seat helpings of the dinner prepared for tonight's feast.

"And now for the most important part: the menu for your din-din. Your meals tonight shall consist of hors d'oeuvres – canned peas and a generous helping of mashed potatoes drenched in gravy, a main course of calf liver – served properly – extra bloody, sans onions and bacon, and my specialty dessert – maple walnut ice cream. You will also be blessed with cranberry juice – straight from the Cape's famous Bog de Atropos – to keep your palates cleansed and moist. I hope you'll enjoy these delicacies. As you can imagine, they were quite costly and difficult for me to obtain. And now, Stefan, please ring the bell in front of you so Philip can begin serving.

Sincerely, Wayne."

At this point, Stefan, using only his thumb and index finger, picked up the small golden bell from the table and rang it ever-so-delicately. The ringing sound it produced was terribly faint, but just loud enough to catch the attention of Philip, who had clearly been lying in wait behind the door to the kitchen. Within a second he emerged, clothed in a black suit with matching bow-tie and cummerbund. He carried with him a large, unwieldy serving tray that held ten small plates of peas and mashed potatoes. The bated eyes around me stared intently and their conditioned tongues began to drool.

While Philip served and I sat at the table, I pondered what caused Wayne's fathers and brothers to appear so absurdly courteous and respectful. I wasn't positive what the agent-of-facade happened to be, but I felt as though it must have involved some kind of extortion, bribery, or blackmail - at the very least. Regardless, I noticed that by the time Philip had dispersed half of the mashed potatoes and peas, the politeness veneer began to show the first signs of cracking. Wayne's family appeared to be undergoing considerable restraint. Normally, they would never consider waiting until each family member had been served. However, just as Gary looked oh-so-very-close to spontaneously com-bust-ing, the last plate of peas and potatoes landed on the table in front of Wayne's vacant chair. There was a momentary relaxation of tension, and then, the dinner officially commenced.

During the consumption of mashed potatoes and peas, there was no talking what-so-ever. All of the men were perfectly focused on their food, which happened to be thoroughly repulsive. It's true, the potatoes were steaming hot, but they were lumpy and sour. The gravy, conversely, was lukewarm and filled with chewy gobs of who-knows-what. And the peas were not only shriveled, but possessed an unhealthy grayish-green tint.

Wayne's family members, however, were of a different opinion: They ate with great speed, efficiency, and gusto. In fact, the bastards worked like machines. They stuffed their mouths with spoonfuls of mashed potatoes and gravy, followed by spoonfuls of peas, and washed that slop down with a gulp or two of cranberry juice. This process was repeated until what once was aplenty was no more. Wayne's family gave no consideration to the idea of saving room in their stomachs for the main course. Fortunately, the treacherous Choppinwood decamped with much of what was on my plate, so I only had to hide a small portion of my food under the table.

At the precise moment the first course was finished, Philip returned, retrieved our empty dishes, and poured all of us some more of that extra-special-extra-tart-cranberry-juice. As he filled our glasses, Nick decided it was time to break the conversational ice, and initiated what he believed to be quite the intellectual discourse about politics, the environment, and several other miscellaneous, hot-button issues. Most notably, he had a mouthful to say about immigration.

"What we, as a people," he said, "require for our safety and economic viability, is the construction of moats - long and wide moats - to keep foreign-shitheads from stepping foot into our country."

"Yes, Nicholas," I added. "That, my friend, is an idea I have yet to hear - both practical and innovative. And it would be relatively inexpensive as well: Two sides are already water. But what should be done about the large number of shitheads who already live in this country legally?"

Immediately after I posed this question, I thought it would be best to keep my observations to myself. I expected a disproportionate backlash, but surprisingly, the only response I received was dead-air.

Luckily, after some tough, silent moments, Stefan changed the subject. I guess Nick's comments proved to be inspirational and motivated Stefan to say something profound. He introduced all of us to another unprecedented idea.

"All these folks," he informed us, "keep whining and clamoring about trash and recycling. To hell with them. I propose we simply load the world's trash into a space-ship and shoot it from the space-ship into the sun. Problem solved."

I couldn't help myself and asked Stefan for clarification.

"Would the rocket return home after the trip," I asked, "so we could get our deposit back?"

Unfortunately, my question was drowned out by additional philosophizing. Wayne's family talked over almost every word I said. I felt slightly ridiculous after my contribution fell so flat.

Finally, Gary assumed control. Not to be out-done, he went a little non-sequitur and launched into a rant about fashion and the importance of "matching hair color to each of the four seasons."

This advice, predictably, brought about a salient silence, which happened to accompany Philip's delivery of the main course: liver.

It should be noted that Philip made a real spectacle of himself on his way from the kitchen and into the dining room. The poor little guy was clearly the underdog as he worked to balance a gigantic, gleaming silver platter and the eight plates of liver on top of it. I counted at least three separate instances when he almost toppled over and dropped our fare onto the dining room floor. Of course, none of us offered him any assistance, despite the fact that all he needed was one helping hand. I suppose we were all far too spellbound. We just watched him and wondered whether or not he would be able to avoid what appeared to be a certain culinary calamity. Philip, however, refused to surrender, and after a nerve-wracking series of seconds, successfully set the tray down on the side table. He then began to deliver the meals with which he had been rightly entrusted.

The distribution of the main course proved to be the greatest stress-inducing event of the dinner. Granted, it only took Philip about a minute to serve the food, but he wasn't nimble enough for Wayne's family. Gary and Nick were especially agitated with the situation. Their faces turned so red with impatience, I thought their heads would pop off and blast through the ceiling. The veins in their necks were alarmingly pronounced and were about to burst and splatter blood everywhere. Wayne's brothers weren't immune to the avidity virus either, and they fidgeted as if trapped inside straitjackets. But, fortunately, just before all-hell-broke-loose, the last plate of liver was placed in front of me. All of us were, once again, greatly relieved – all of us except for Choppinwood, my dining table next-door-neighbor. For reasons unknown to me at the time, he was not presented with a meal of any kind.

The fried chunk of calf liver positioned on the plate in front of me looked like the de-feathered carcass of an obese pigeon. Disgustingly enough, it was both under and overcooked at the same time – the worst and worst of tough and tender. The thin part was well-well-done, fibrous, and slightly burnt. The thick portion was undercooked and contained bits and pieces that were still raw. Most interestingly, the meat was also awash in a curious, anti-appetizing pool of maroon colored juices.

This time, it came as no surprise to me that Wayne's fathers and brothers chowed down on that shit like there would be no tomorrow. Still, despite the fact I knew those manly men would eat anything put in front of them, it was rather shocking to watch them devour their food like such savages. They ate so damned quickly they didn't even take the time to wipe that maroon mystery sauce off their faces. I just sat there and watched as it trickled from their mouths, down their chins, and back onto their plates. If not for the suits they wore, I don't think I could have picked them out of a line-up of rabid, cannibalistic monsters.

During the main course, it became quite clear to me why Choppinwood was denied his fair share of calf liver. The reason was certainly odd, but quite simple: While Wayne's family members fed upon the meat in front of them, they emitted, one at a time, a juicy-kind-of-clicking sound into the air. Whenever this off-putting noise was created, Choppinwood's head popped up, as if he were shocked by a small primate prod. Then, the capuchin marauder ran feverishly toward the source of the click. Without even looking at the devious animal, a piece of dinner was dangled by an outstretched hand and quickly inhaled, gobbled up, and annihilated. This process was repeated throughout our bovine supper and caused the frenzied Choppinwood to zigzag across the table, diner to diner. In order to make whatever-that-shit was on my plate disappear, I even got in on the action and beckoned Choppinwood, by click, several times. Interestingly enough, it seems that Wayne's family reserves this clicking tradition for main courses, as it did not occur during the appetizer.

As for what exactly transpired during dessert, well, the answer to that is complex and possibly impossible to explain. All I know for certain is that I fell into some type of delirium – an unsettling, unique variety of hallucinogenic daze. It must have been that damned cranberry juice from the bogs of the Cape that did it to me, because I didn't consume much of anything else during dinner. In addition, whatever Wayne or Philip deposited in my drink was, beyond a doubt, present in the rest of the beverages on the dining table. I'm sure of this fact due to the frightful and bizarre series of actions that ensued – full tilt – that night. Besides, I would like to think that human-beings aren't capable of acting in such a manner - unless drugged to lose complete sense and sensibility.

My last completely lucid memory of dinner involves Philip as he delicately laid a sizable helping of maple walnut ice cream onto the plate in front of me. Moments after that, a ray of light reflected off the silver colored dessert dish and entered my eye at an uncommon, uncomfortable, and unexpected angle. It's true, I'm quite sure I would have experienced my surreal visions and dizzying delirium anyhow, but I feel as if that beam of artificial light served as a catalyst. It must have been partly responsible for throwing my harrowing, yet absurd, experience into motion. After that emanation made contact with my eyeball, I was, almost immediately, struck with an intense headache, a strong feeling of nausea, and the perception that my pupils had become as wide as flying saucers. I tried to speak several times, but either couldn't, or slurred my words and said something that sounded completely nonsensical. I thought my dinner colleagues would have noticed my abrupt change in demeanor, but they paid no attention to me. Undoubtedly, they had already fallen victim to the tainted cranberry juice.

It was at this juncture of the evening that the hand hallucinations began. I recall that my head was in great pain, and I was, for no particular reason, staring fixedly and feverishly ahead at some floral patterned wallpaper on the opposite wall. I blinked for a millisecond, opened my eyes, and saw that a floating, phantasmal palm and fingers had morphed out of the woodwork. I blinked a couple more times, as if the specter would disappear, but it remained there – hovering two-thirds of the way up the wall. After a good thirty seconds, the apparition then reversed itself one hundred and eighty degrees, formed into a fist, and released a long, skinny middle finger into the air.

That's when the writing commenced. The tip of the middle finger pressed itself against the wall and slowly smeared a blood-red message on top of some brugmansia flowers. I watched in between the heads of Jean and Stefan as each letter was added from right to left. When the middle finger finished its proclamation, I couldn't tell whether its words were extremely cryptic and enigmatic, or absolutely foolish and indecipherable. But there, on the wall, was a message - a message I believe may have been meant for me.

Regrettably, I can only remember bits and pieces of the bloody bulletin.

I'm fairly certain it ended with these words:

"It does, because it is."

Before that, though, I'm at a bit of a loss.
It's conceivable it said something like:

**"They put gall in my food and gave
me vinegar for my thirst."**

It's also possible the message simply stated:

"Doughnuts make my brown eyes blue."

To my disbelief, no one else at the table noticed the finger as it wrote on the wall. Instead, Wayne's family was wholly engaged in a violent, unruly argument about the amount of maple walnut ice cream and the lack of a second serving. The manly crew was completely incensed and channeled their rage toward an innocent and relatively defenseless scapegoat: Philip. The moving finger continued to write and Serge began to chase Philip around the table. I'm pretty sure if Philip had been caught that night, he would've been consumed raw. Luckily, though, just as it appeared

Philip was trapped in the corner of the dining room, he managed to run between Yann's legs, into the hallway, and straight out the back door of the house. Apparently, twelve-year-olds, when pushed to the brink, can be exceptionally dexterous and are capable of extraordinary feats of athleticism.

The pursuit of Philip and the accompanying theatrics provided perfect cover for me to abscond unharmed. Despite the pain in my brain, and an outrageously queasy feeling in my stomach, I managed to get up from my seat at the table and exit through the front door. I did look back, however, just before I disappeared into the night. I peered into the dining room, and, I swear, I saw a bloodied figure sitting in Wayne's formerly empty seat. I did a double take, of course, but the grisly shape was gone. I'm not sure if the figure was a ghostly version of Wayne, or the infernal Choppinwood. My eye-sight just isn't what it used to be.

"I caught Wayne once. It was around the holidays and he was working as a temporary letter carrier for the post office. I saw him on his route and he tossed something or other into a catch basin. I wasn't sure what he threw, but I had my suspicions, so I followed him. He turned the corner to another street and he placed his mail bag to the pavement. Then, he sat down on the curb between his bag and another catch basin. That's when he started to remove what appeared to be gift catalogues and large magazines. He took them, one by one, and stuffed them down into the catch basin. I suppose he thought his bag was too heavy.

The second I got home I called the post office and reported what I witnessed. Wayne was fired. I called the post office a week later - just to be sure."

-PRISCILLA DRINKWATER

CHAPTER 24

Barrie's Concerns

———————

I'M NOT SURE HOW I arrived home. I suppose it's most likely I stumbled, hobbled, and staggered all the way to the pool-house on my own two feet. I do know, however, that it was still dark when I appeared at my door. It must have been somewhere between midnight and 3:00 a.m.

I took the key to the pool-house from my pocket and tried to open the door, but it wouldn't budge. That's when I noticed that the door plate was a different color than usual - a forest green - and the keyhole was bright red. It looked like it was on fire. I tried to get in and fiddled with the lock for what felt like hours, but it must have only been a couple of minutes. Eventually, my key turned red - to match the keyhole - and I was good to go.

There wasn't a single light on in the pool-house, which was a relief. My head ached and I was still extra-sensitive - allergic - to anything shiny or luminescent. The lack of light, though, was part of Barrie's plan to catch me by surprise. He must have put plenty of thought into the scene he designed.

And his plan somewhat worked, I guess, because I didn't even notice him until I was half-way through the kitchen.

"Barry," his composed, yet menacing voice said. "Now, Barry. You've had a long, long evening. Haven't you?"

My eyes instantly shifted toward my interrogator. I looked up and across the kitchen and found Barrie. He was sitting on top of the refrigerator. One of his legs was propped between the fridge door and the fridge itself. As a result of this maneuver, his miniature body was highlighted in eerie incandescent light. The effect reminded me of kids who stick flashlights under their chins to illuminate their masks on Halloween.

"Do you think you can just march on in here whenever you please?" he inquired. "You have a curfew."

"Why do you have to be so dramatic, Barrie?" I asked. "What kind of person ambushes someone from atop a refrigerator in the middle of the night?"

"Don't turn this on me, you double-dealing fiend!" he said belligerently.

"How long have you been waiting up there with your leg like that? That must be pretty uncomfortable."

"What were you doing without me tonight!" he screamed in his innocent-toddler, ventriloquist dummy voice.

"That's none of your concern," I said. "Stop acting like a fucking psycho."

This comment greatly upset Barrie and caused him to vault from the top of the refrigerator and sprint toward me, crying, at full speed. I could tell he meant business. He carried a butter knife in each hand and his shaggy, mop-top hair-do bounced up and down, all around. It was quite terrifying.

I ran for the front door and opened it as swiftly as possible. Luckily, I made it outside just in time. I slammed the door shut and heard a thud when Barrie smacked straight into it. The miniature man was so excited he must have misjudged his speed and couldn't stop in time. I put my ear to the door and listened closely, but I heard nothing. He probably knocked himself out cold.

"Religion? The opiate of the masses? Not any longer.
It's sports - football in particular - if you ask me.
Maybe a little religion sprinkled here and there."

-DR. DRINKWATER

CHAPTER 25

End of a Slumber: The Shitty News

———

THE NEXT DAY, I FOUND myself in the HMS Talbot, floating in the middle of the pool. It was fairly hot outside and the sun looked to be directly overhead. Fortunately, a large towel covered my face and most of my body. I can't remember if I applied the towel myself or if a strange guardian angel was responsible for the deed. It's possible that Barrie did so out of guilt - a peace offering after his bizarre and violent melt-down.

I'm somewhat certain I didn't rise naturally from my slumber. Specifically, I believe that someone threw a stone into the pool - possibly several stones, for that matter - in order to wake me. Not only did part of my pant leg have fresh water droplets on it, but when I removed the towel from my face, something moved quickly and rustled in the bushes. Whatever the case, I stuck one of my arms into the water and casually hand-paddled my way to the steps in the shallow-end.

When I got to the pool-house door I found that it was unlocked and, therefore, didn't require any key jiggling or fidgeting. I opened it a crack and checked to see if any danger lurked in and around the kitchen appliances. Fortunately, I saw no evidence of Barrie and what transpired a handful of hours ago. In any case - just to be on the safe side - I grabbed my plastic, yellow wiffle ball bat and surreptitiously searched the premises. Barrie, thankfully, was nowhere to be found - all was clear. I wondered if I'd ever see that dummy again.

Anyhow, after I searched the house, I decided to go outside and join the buzzing world. The second I opened the front door, though, I saw something - someone - fumbling in the bushes. Whatever it was, it was small and disappeared before I knew it. I was about to give chase, but realized that would be a fruitless endeavor. Instead, my eyes caught something out of the ordinary at my feet: a manila envelope, half-tucked underneath the welcome mat. Inside of it were two items. The first, was a note that said:

"Read this, shit-for-brains."

The second, was a newspaper article about a car that exploded by the side of the highway. It was titled "Fiery Flames by the Breakdown Lane."

FIERY FLAMES BY THE BREAKDOWN LANE:
CONGESTION OF A CENTRAL ARTERY

Needles, Mass – A car explosion and subsequent fire on Route 128 North required one-and-a-half fire engines earlier this morning. The accident occurred near Exit 33B and resulted in the closure of two lanes for approximately one hour and forty-five minutes.

Authorities are uncertain of the victim's identity, as the body was burned beyond recognition. Investigators are, admittedly, puzzled over what caused the crash and massive fire.

Larry Wilcox, a state policeman who was the third to arrive at the scene, says he believes sudden and dense patches of fog may be to blame. "Yeah," he said, "this fog came out of nowhere when I was on patrol early this morning. I bet the driver of the vehicle encountered some of it. Drove off the road in confusion. Hit that boulder. Car exploded. End of story."

Luckily, the accident was early enough in the morning and only had a minimal impact on the morning commute. "Yeah, could have been worse," Sgt. Wilcox explained. "Could have been a lot worse. Still, the curiosity factor definitely slowed down a good number of folks headed southbound."

Orval Billingtons, a local pediatrician, was the first to encounter the fiery catastrophe. "I came after the collision," he said. "There were flames everywhere. Never seen anything quite like it. Nothing I could do."

"I spent nine months or so in another person's body and I don't remember a single second of it."

-WAYNE

CHAPTER 26A

Return to Spit-House

———•———

AFTER I READ THE CRASH REPORT, I immediately made my way over to the House of Wayne, also known as Spit-House. I rang the bell and waited at the front door for several minutes, but no one answered. I even walked down the drive-way and into the backyard, but I couldn't find evidence of present life. Frustrated, I returned to the front yard and sought some unlawful-entry re-assurance from Bathtub-Mary. After I received her blessing, I approached the front door and tried the knob. Miraculously, it was unlocked. I then looked over my shoulder, suspiciously-guiltily, and entered the dwelling as an uninvited intruder.

I was on my toes the entire time I searched through the House of Wayne, also known as Spit-House. I knew if caught inside, there was a good chance Gary, Nick, or one of Wayne's brothers, would utilize reasonable means to eliminate me. Still, my curiosity overrode staying within the practical bounds of my "comfort zone."

I wanted to ease into trespassing, so I tossed myself a soft-ball task: I inspected the living room first - a result of my severe approach-avoidance issues. As expected, there wasn't much action in there, aside from the creaking noises my footsteps created. Although, I should note the room was actually quite pleasing to behold. It was drenched with sun and the polished-looking floor-boards gleamed in the light. There was also a peaceful-still feeling - a feeling the continuous revolutions of the two ceiling fans added to, rather than detracted.

After the calm before the storm, it came time for the real crime scene investigation, so I discreetly-silently crossed the hall-way and entered the dining room. As expected, it was a mess. Chairs were scattered here and there and the table was littered with dirty dishes, broken, near-empty glasses, and tarnished sil-verware everywhere the eye could see. The linens were also cov-ered with amoeba-shaped cranberry juice stains - but there wasn't an extra crumb to be found. Choppinwood, the monkey-vacuum, probably returned to the scene of the crime and consumed any remaining bits and morsels. I scanned the walls for bloody graf-fiti, but I only found floral wall-paper. What once was, was no more - or - what once wasn't, remained so.

It was at this point that I realized it was probably time to go. I started to ask myself what I was doing and I couldn't come up with a good answer. It was just as I was about to leave when I thought of something: Wayne's basement living quarters.

The second I opened the cellar door, I knew I was meant to explore the dark, dank basement. Instantly, I heard music which played ever so softly and echoed lightly throughout the subter-ranean room. I couldn't decipher the words at first, but I could hear synthesizers at work and what sounded like a drum machine.

When I reached the bottom of the stairs, the song was clearer. I'm pretty sure the lyrics I heard involved taking away another person's breath.

Surprisingly, I became somewhat emotional when I saw Stinky-Winky, that solitary Red-Tele-Tubby. It appeared so lonely sitting at the table, accompanied by no one - except for two empty chairs. That music sure was effective, too. In fact, I was so taken with the set-up and the ambience, it took me a moment to realize something unusual: Stinky-Winky held an envelope with my name on it between his mitts. I had been looking directly at it, but neglected to see it.

I picked the envelope up, opened it, and found it contained a letter from Wayne. It said the following:

Dearest Barry,

You found this letter. Good job. You may take a two-minute break to relax and collect your thoughts.

Okay, the two-minute break has come to an end.

Now that you've relaxed, I will provide you with directions for your next task.

They're simple:

1. Go to the Needles Public Library.
2. Find the biography section.
3. Locate an *authorized* biography of the Dalai Lama (I think it's titled 'Man, Monk, Mystic.')
4. Turn to page sixty-nine.
5. There, you will find something special.

Sincerely,
Wayne

p.s. - Don't get your naughty bits in a bunch. This is not a wild goose chase, as you like to say. Sometimes, there's a method to the madness, as you also like to say.

CHAPTER 26B

Escape from Spit-House

———◆———

AFTER I READ WAYNE'S LETTER, I muttered "what an ass-hole" under my breath and shoved it into my pocket. Understandably, I was mildly annoyed and under a bit of pressure. I had definitely overstayed my un-welcome and was tempting fate, dilly-dallying in the basement. Undoubtedly, it was high-time to withdraw from the House of Wayne, also known as Spit-House.

When I turned to head up the stairs, though, Choppinwood entered the picture. He looked me in the eyes for a second and charged down the hazardous wooden steps at me screeching like a belligerent bird. His mouth was open wide, and his arms and tail waved wildly in the air. He jumped right at my head - as expected - but I managed to parry his attack and swatted the wily bastard away from my face. He hit the boiler and landed awkwardly on the concrete floor. I immediately gunned it up the stairs and slammed the door behind me. Seconds later, I heard Choppinwood running up the steps after me in one of his monkey-furors. All of this was too much for me, and induced post-traumatic flashbacks of the previous night's altercation with Barrie.

I knew I had to move fast. Choppinwood has always been a cagey mother-fucker and I was quite aware that a cellar door wouldn't stymie him for long. Accordingly, I ran to a window that overlooked the front yard to see if the coast was clear - which I considered to be an unusually thoughtful maneuver during such stressful times. Of course, not to my surprise, I saw Wayne's dads as they exited their car at the tip of the drive-way. The two of them must have forgotten something at the house - I'm not sure.

For some reason, I kind of froze and just watched as Gary and Nick approached the front door. I don't know what was wrong with me for a couple of seconds - maybe I somewhat wanted to be caught. Fortunately, though, I snapped out of my daze while I watched a spit-in-action. Two people in a car happened to slowly approach and stop their vehicle in front of The House of Wayne, also known as Spit-House. The individual on the passenger side leaned out the car window and spat on the walkway in the front yard - a direct hit. Gary and Nick turned exactly in time to see the saliva splash onto the cement. Incensed, they took off after the spitter and his accomplice, yelling and swearing - a real spectacle.

I took advantage of this timely development, ran to the back door, and followed Philip's proven escape route. I jumped over a rusty fence and some shrubbery, and found myself a few feet from the squirrel fountain in Mr. Appleton's backyard. I then took the opportunity to gaze upon the bubbling water, just as Wayne did back at the end of August. I watched carefully for a fair amount of time as the water traveled from level to level, and the squirrels twirled and performed pirouettes. Eventually, I felt the need to urinate into the fountain, but I suppressed the urge. I didn't want

Mr. Appleton to catch me in the act and have me arrested for a bizarre sex crime. The last thing I want is one of those on my record.

Alas, I didn't have any particular place to go, so I followed Wayne's pain-in-the-ass instructions and traveled to Needles Public Library. It was the least I could do to ensure life remained entertaining.

"The more time I spend trying to delete myself from the world, the more alive I feel. I guess you could say it's kind of like a sine wave relationship."

-WAYNE

CHAPTER 27

Needles Public Library

———

IT TOOK ME FIFTEEN MINUTES or so to walk from the House of Wayne, also known as Spit-House, to the Needles Public Library. The place is open until 5:00 p.m. on Fridays, so I had a decent amount of time to spare. It's a nice library - a Gothic Revival building - that was built in 1915 at the bequest of some rich bastard. The facade is impressive and boasts a brick walkway, which leads to two sets of steps on either side of a stone portico. Patrons can opt to go left or right, but will end up at the same front door - regardless of their selection.

I entered the library and got to my assignment immediately, an unlikely turn of events for me. I walked past the circulation desk, the fiction room, and took the stairs to the second floor. I then proceeded to the right and walked by stacks and stacks of library books. And there, in the last aisle, were two sights of particular note: the B-for-Biography section and a suspicious someone sitting in a chair by the window. This particular person was reading a newspaper that conveniently blocked his or her face.

It took me longer than it should have to find *Dalai Lama: Man, Monk, Mystic*. The newspaper clown made me nervous.

I glanced over each time I thought I saw the paper slide downward - only to see it immediately return to its original position. In addition, some discourteous ding-a-ling placed *Man, Monk, Mystic* in the wrong place. Never-the-less, I pressed onward and found the book. It was, as Wayne said, totally *authorized*, written with the Lama's complete cooperation.

I shot a look at the curious stranger, the newspaper went up, and I opened the book in search of page sixty-nine. There, between pages sixty-eight and seventy, I found yet another envelope with my name on it. Inside the envelope, was a letter which contained Wayne's "autoeulogy" and a request that I deliver it at his funeral. I wasn't sure that Wayne had actually died, but I guess his autoeulogy somewhat confirmed the notion. Also, I have to say Wayne may have been more eloquent than I thought, although the words of his autoeulogy do seem to be somewhat familiar.

The letter went as follows:

My Dearest Barry,

If you're reading this letter, then surely a terrible tragedy has befallen me and my body no longer walks upon the surface of our Earth.

Please understand: I have always wanted to write a sentence like the sentence above this one and I could not resist the rare opportunity to do so.

Alas, due to the circumstances, I have arranged some words for you to recite to the souls-in-mourning who attend my funeral.

It is of the utmost importance that you read my autoeulogy exactly as I have prescribed. The moments of dead-air were carefully concocted to maximize the poignancy of the situation - my words plus my passing.

I have a feeling the emotional impact will be substantial. I wouldn't be surprised if some attendees fall victim to the sorrowful vapors that will saturate the air and envelope the service. "Gut-wrenching," as you like to say.

Do not tell anyone this is an autoeulogy.

Take credit for the beauty of my words.

Sincerely yours,
Best Friends Forever,
Wayne

P.S. - You may have to rehearse this a couple of times beforehand. In other words, make sure not to fuck it up and read like a monotone robot.
P.P.S. - My balls are in your court now.

Instructions for Barry (My Autoeulogy):

1. Slowly approach the podium.
2. Do not make eye contact with the crowd.
3. Use your right hand and take the autoeulogy from your front-left-inner-breast pocket.
4. Set the autoeulogy on the podium.
5. Put each of your hands on either side of the podium.
6. Look down and count to thirty-three.
7. Cough three times. Clear your throat.
8. Say the following:
   "His name was Wayne. We met at a confectionery shoppe."
   "Everyone told me he came from the bad part of town, the wrong side of the rails."
9. Count to 6.9.
   "But he knew the country like a fox or a bird.
   He knew every track in the snow or on the ground, and what creature had taken his path before him."
9. Stop. Pause for effect. Wait 6.9 seconds.
10. Say the following and act as if you are on the verge of crying:
    "His riddles were worth the reading, and I confide that, if at any time I do not understand the expression, it is yet just."
11. Count to 6.9.
12. Say the following:

"Thus, it seems an injury that he should leave in the midst his broken task, which none else can finish."

13. Wipe your left eye with a pocket square.

14. Count to 6.9.

15. Say the following:
"But he, at least, is content."

16. Count to 6.9.

17. Say the following:
"His soul was made for the noblest society and he, unfortunately, had in a short life exhausted the capabilities of this world."

18. Count to 6.9.

19. Say the following:
"When he sped off on that foggy-late-night, I told him to drive safely. But he was in a rush. He had appointments to keep, places to be, people to see."

20. Say the following and appear weepy once more:
"I brought my hands to my head and covered my face. There was no way to intervene, his momentum couldn't be stopped. All I could do was think of the good times we shared. They came back to me in flashes."

21. Count to 6.9.

22. Close with these words:
"And now, all that's left to say is:
Wherever there is knowledge,
Wherever there is virtue,
Wherever there is beauty,

He will find a home.
It was a pleasure and a privilege to walk with him.
The country knows not yet, or in the least part, how great
a son it has lost."
23. Fade out.

Just as I read instruction twenty-three, the spy in the chair
jumped up and dashed into the labyrinthine stacks. I probably
should have given chase, but I let the rascal go - and, by doing
so, brought an end to Friday's adventure. I have to admit - at that
point, without any further directives, I wasn't sure what to do
with myself.

"You have to learn to accept a person for the small percentage of him that you like, and ignore the gigantic percentage of him you find totally reprehensible."

-Dr. Drinkwater

CHAPTER 28

The Wake

———◆———

THE WAKE DIDN'T TAKE PLACE until two weeks after the catastrophic crash, explosion, and uncontrollable fire. A cursory investigation ruled out the more likely explanations for the accident, and instead chose to focus on asinine theories that led nowhere. In the end, what happened by **Exit 33B** was forgotten rather quickly due to incompetence, poor effort, and most importantly, a lack of general concern. The powers-that-be were just plain unable, or unwilling, to satisfactorily pinpoint the circumstances behind Wayne's fateful crash.

I thought there would be a crowd of mourners assembled for Wayne's wake at Turlington Funeral Home. After all, he was relatively young when he met his demise and he had an extended family comprised of tragedy lovers. But I was wrong. When I arrived toward the end of visitation hours, I was one of only a few guests present and the third caller to sign the guestbook. Signature number one was mostly illegible, but I could tell the first and last names began with an S. The name above mine looked familiar - Calvin Turlington - but that mystery was immediately solved. A guy about my age crept up from behind me and tapped me on the shoulder.

"Yeah, that's my name above yours," he said in hushed tones. "Saw you looking at it. I work here. I noticed folks weren't too interested in the guestbook, so I signed it. Felt bad. I knew Wayne a long time ago. Haven't seen him in years."

I nodded in agreement and was rewarded with a prayer card that he handed me. I nodded once more, appreciatively, and sat down in a Victorian ladies parlor chair to study the double-sided card. The first side I looked at included a poorly drawn illustration of Sister Mary and these words:

Psalm 69

I am a stranger to my brothers, an alien to my own mother's sons.

Those who sit at the gate mock me, and I am the song of drunkards.

The reverse side contained a head shot of Wayne with pinkish-purple laser beams in the background. Underneath that - his high school portrait - was the Alcoholics Anonymous version of the Serenity Prayer.

After I read the double-sided prayer card, I begrudgingly made my way toward the visitation room. On the way, I passed a large bulletin board filled with photographs of Wayne. Most - if not all - of the photos captured his brothers as they tortured him. They pulled at his hair in one photo and suffocated him with a pillow in another. The best photo – the most sentimental one, in my opinion – featured Wayne's brothers as they smothered his face in freshly fallen snow. His family failed to realize it, but all of the images served as perfect evidence of Wayne's prolonged mental and physical suffering. His brothers, though, looked genuinely happy in those photos. In fact, they were having so much fun, they probably thought Wayne enjoyed being tormented and brutalized in such a playful manner.

When I finally reached the visitation room, I took a moment to behold the receiving line – a line that was difficult to decipher due to the unusual number of identical humans. I know for sure that Choppinwood was at the front of it, then - I think - it went from Gervais, to Yann, to Jean, to Serge, to Stefan, to Nick, and finally, to Gary, who stood closest to the casket. Choppinwood wore a tuxedo-shirt, and the quintuplet brothers were clothed in moth-holed t-shirts with mustard-looking stains, distressed jeans, and beige-brown work boots. Gary and Nick were dressed in their state police uniforms - they must have come straight from work.

Before the five of them saw me, I could hear Wayne's brothers grumbling to Gary and Nick. They were upset about the length of the wake and they were tired of standing. When their eyes found me, however, they stopped their childish whining and their faces morphed into tough-guy-scowl configurations. I knew it would be difficult to pass by the one-rowed, pseudo grief-gauntlet, but I saw no alternatives.

I thought of hugging Choppinwood, but I knew it would be best to ignore the perfidious primate. He was giving me the hairy-skunk eye, which probably meant he remembered the boiler and basement door incident. I'm sure he was frustrated that he couldn't tell Wayne's family what happened.

I then saw Gervais spit in his hands and rub them together before we shook. I said "I'm so sorry," facetiously, and moved down the line to Yann, who happened to be mid-yawn when I got to him. I took advantage of the situation.

"Some of my thoughts are with you," I said, and managed to get by him without any physical contact.

As for Jean, I stood in front of him for too long. Neither of us said anything. We just stared with ill intent into one another's eyes. Eventually, after a less than elegant moment together, I gave up on any verbal interaction and stepped over to Serge.

Serge looked rather smug.

"I'ham so glahd yah could make it," he informed me, with a half insane look on his face.

He then jerked his arm forward to shake my hand. When our hands grasped one another, he extended his pointer finger and forcefully stroked the bottom of my wrist. For whatever reason, he really enjoyed the opportunity to fondle my radial artery.

"Don't worry, I'm here for you," I falsely confessed, thinking a comment, any comment, would end our palm to palm synergy.

Thankfully, those insincere words did the trick and I regained autonomy over my arm and hand. Still, I felt defiled and disgusted with myself.

When I got to Stefan, he grabbed my hand and pulled me forward until we were chest to chest. Then, he placed his chin on my shoulder. I suppose he intended to create the illusion of a shared, heartfelt moment.

"Now I know why yah wearing that fahhkin homo-suit," he whispered into my ear. "Next time we'ahh alone I'm going to rip yah fahhkin heart outtah yah chest and eat it right in front-ah yah. Understand, mah-thah fahkah?"

I backed away from Stefan.

"Yes, I understand," I said. "I know you're having a tough time right now. Those are some great photos, by the way. Did you prefer being the cameraman or the strangler?"

Stefan half-smiled and threatened me again with his eyes. I moved on to Wayne's dads.

Luckily, Gary and Nick were talking to one another and didn't hear me ask Stefan the photo question. I shook their hands.

"Sorry for your loss," I said. "Wayne was a good friend."

I could tell they didn't want anything to do with me, though. They offered up a "thanks fah coming," but I knew what they really meant to say was:

"Don't mess with us. It's time for you to get the fuck out of here."

Finally, I made it to Wayne's casket. I thought it would be completely closed, but I soon found otherwise. The bottom was shut, but the upper half was wide open. And, right where Wayne's face should have been, was the head of his red tele-tubby costume. I almost laughed out loud - nervously - but Gary spoke up.

"That's tha only true friend ah Wayne's we know aahhv," he explained. "It was his bra-thas' idea tah put it in there. As yah know, his body bahrned to bits."

Then, Gary added some important words.

"And now I'd like all of-yahs to bow yah heads and listen to a po-em I found in tha basement," he said. "A friend ah-mine at work told me it appears to have three quatrains and ah couplet – whatevah they ahh. All I know is it was written by Wayne. I think he wrote it shortly before he died. I'd like yah all to listen as I read his beautiful, but harhd to un-dah-stand words."

At that moment, Gary began to read aloud and enunciate perfectly.

"I now present to you a poem, by my son, a boy named Wayne," he informed us. "It goes like this:

Sonnet 33B

On this road's exit in which they play,
My curiosity, like a raptor, eagerly waits.
Watching there - where all the car parts lay -
Encircling constantly, my mind debates.
Ofttimes I lurk - when fate places luck in my mitts,
And grasp its treasure - found in this rotary.
Soon then my bit of fortune revolves and flits,
I inquire and find the cave by gyres a comedy.
This vent, mesmerizing me with its awful eye,
Turns not in my sight, nor loves my art.
But when I explore, it inhales - and when I sigh,
It storms and etches forever so smart.
Where then can I find it? If it's wind that's thrown?
This is no Lechuguilla, but a sentient blown."

With that, Gary concluded reading the sonnet that was supposedly written by Wayne. He didn't say another word. There was no crying whatsoever in the room. There was only the strongest feeling of confusion I've ever encountered. It's true - I was a bit miffed that Wayne received credit for my poem, but I knew it was neither the time nor the place to say anything. I also knew that time and place would never exist.

I left Turlington Funeral Home as Wayne's brothers discussed the words they thought he composed. As I exited the visitation room, I heard them say:

"That poem sucked,"

"Poetry is fah fags,"

and

"Fahk Wayne."

With an understanding look on his face, Calvin Turlington graciously opened the front door for me and I nodded once again. It felt good to be released and reacquainted with the night-time air. I leaned against a street-light for a minute or so. Then, I ambled on home.

"Conspiracy theories? I guess the first one that comes to mind has to do with seahorses. It's ridiculous, if you ask me. I just don't know why the government insists on telling us the male seahorse gives birth. What do they have to gain? It's fucking preposterous."

-WAYNE

CHAPTER 29

The Funeral

WAYNE'S FUNERAL TOOK PLACE ON a windy, crisp, and desolate afternoon at St. Mary's, the day after his wake. I have to admit I was a wee-bit tardy when I entered the brick Romanesque Revival church. The service was well under way and the priest was wrapping up his comments about the after-life and the deceased. He said something about sin, death, and the possibility of mercy - a few of Wayne's favorite things. Then, the preacher called upon me.

"Is there a Barry Drinkwater here?" he inquired. "A Barry Drinkwater? I've been instructed that a Mr. Barry Drinkwater is to provide the eulogy."

I raised my hand and walked up to the lectern at the front of the church. I looked out and over the pews - at my temporary congregation - and saw that there were slightly more people present than I had expected. Wayne's dads, his brothers, and Choppinwood occupied two of the front pews and were lined up in the same order they assumed for the wake. The extras in the audience were scattered here and there in the middle. I figured they were regular church-goers who enjoy being part of the death ceremony experience. However, I did notice two familiar, home-less faces / town of Needles representatives: Tracey the Bag Lady and her on and off again boyfriend, Moon Man Muldoon. Their eyes weren't focused on me, rather they were pointed down-ward toward their hands in their laps. Due to their reputation and shifty movements, it dawned on me that they were probably packing cigarettes with weed.

Then, seconds before I began Wayne's autoeulogy, a conspic-uous fellow entered the church. He was tall, somewhat thin, and wore a perfectly black suit - topped off with a matching bowler hat, pushed firmly down upon his head. His most notable char-acteristics, however, were on his face, which was decorated with a handlebar mustache and a chin puff beard. He refused to make eye contact with anyone and sat alone in the last pew closest to the door.

After he took his seat, I removed Wayne's autoeulogy from my front-left-inner-breast pocket and set it on the podium. I then put my hands on either side of the wooden stand and decided - at precisely that moment - that I'd actually try to read the autoeu-logy exactly as Wayne requested. I looked down, counted to thirty-three, coughed three times, and cleared my throat.

I spoke into the microphone.

"His name was Wayne," I confidently stated. "We met at a confectionery shoppe."

No one thought that comment was peculiar. The entire place was silent. It's likely my people weren't listening or needed more context, so I continued as instructed.

"Everyone told me he came from the bad part of town, the wrong side of the rails."

This comment semi-awoke Wayne's sleeping brothers. They were half-listening - at best - before, but at this point their interest was partly piqued. It was when I made the next statement, however, that I realized I might be in for a bit of trouble. Apparently, the idea that Wayne knew the country like a "fox or a bird" rubbed them the wrong way, as did his unlikely ability to identify tracks "in the snow." As soon as I finished that sentence, the autoeulogy became interactive and Wayne's brothers began to add some sophomoric commentary. From there on in, I was a sitting duck up there. Only a podium separated me from the unruly, boorish bunch.

Right after I proclaimed - on the verge of requested tears - that Wayne's "riddles were worth the reading," I heard someone call me a "pussy" under his breath, and some muffled hyena-like chuckling. Soon after that, my right shoulder was struck with a spit-ball, which bounced off me and landed in some sympathy flowers on the floor. I glanced at Wayne's brothers to suggest that they suspend their harassment, but they, collectively, played the innocent fool. That's when I looked toward the dark stranger and saw that he was staring straight back at me. I can't say this for sure, but it looked as if his hypnotic eyes commanded me to:

"Stay strong. Continue with conviction."

He was definitely a master of powerful, telepathic suggestion.

Dutifully, I recited another line of the autoeulogy and wiped my left eye with a pocket square. I told my parishioners that Wayne "is content," his "soul was made for the noblest society," and that he had "exhausted the capabilities of this world." I paid no heed to the brothers' evil eyes and the two additional spit balls that struck my left elbow and my right temple, respectively but disrespectfully. After a pause, I added that I warned Wayne to drive safely when he sped off into the "foggy-late-night."

Then, I produced some semi-real tears and told my people, my flock, there was no time to "intervene," that "Wayne's momentum couldn't be stopped," and all I could do was "think of the good times we had" the night he departed from this world. It was just as I read the next line, and said the word "flashes," that one of Wayne's brothers - most likely Stefan - performed a loud, socially unacceptable bodily function. Vapors were released, but not the type Wayne intended to inspire. In response, a select group were in a state of joy and ecstasy, most were horrified, and some didn't notice at all.

At this point, when all seemed derailed and headed toward chaos, a voice commandeered use of the church address system and uttered some unexpected words.

"Listen, my children," the voice instructed us, "Wayne is not dead. He only sleepeth."

It was a strange voice, broadcasted with plenty of reverb - perhaps the sound a boy would make if he wanted to impersonate an older man. The church fell silent, except for the pitter-patter of footsteps from somewhere above our heads.

I knew I had to take advantage of the silence and finish the autoeulogy. I moved my face close to the microphone and spoke all of the remaining lines, but the last. Then, I paused for almost seven seconds.

"The country knows not yet," I said, "or in the least part, how great a son it has lost."

Immediately following these words, the organist began to play the very same Bach prelude - in F-Minor - that Wayne blared that night on the way to Needles Cemetery. As the gloomy notes filled in around us, I surveyed the audience and saw that no one was weeping as Wayne foresaw. The closest to tears was Gary, whose eyes turned nine percent misty. The rest of his family and "friends" were just too apathetic to express sorrow. I suppose some thought the words I spoke may have been intended for someone other than Wayne. Then again, their lack of emotion may have been because Wayne never fully developed as a person, a character. Few really knew him and fewer had reason to relate to him.

Anyhow, the organ music was my cue to step down and head to the burial. I left as quickly and as discreetly as possible. I'm pretty sure I was the second person out the front door of the church.

"I was with Wayne the day he started to tell people he was 'going pre-med.' Some pretentious fuck was talking to us. Said he was pre-med, on his way to become a doctor, when clearly he was a pompous-full-of-shit-prick. That's when I saw Wayne perk up as if someone stuck him in the ass with a thumbtack. I could actually read his thoughts during that moment. The words might as well have appeared on his forehead. He said to himself: 'Yeah, that sounds about right. I think I'm going pre-med. After all, if one really thinks about it, everyone is pre-med - technically speaking - so I might as well tell the world I'm pre-med too.'"

-BARRY DRINKWATER

CHAPTER 30

The Burial

———

THE WAY THINGS WERE GOING, I expected Wayne's burial to be a vulgar, rowdy, and unhinged spectacle - the icing on the cake, as they say. On the walk to Needles Cemetery, I imagined his internment would feature elements similar to an over-the-top action movie: machine gun battles, air to surface missiles, and a massive rescue operation that would result in Wayne's resuscitation. None of that, however, occurred. His burial was markedly anticlimactic and absent of any further tom-foolery. After all, there was no body to breathe life into, only ashes.

I passed through the cemetery gates after the funeral procession arrived, about a half an hour before sunset. When I got close to Wayne's grave, I found a granite mausoleum to lean against, which was a safe distance away from the action. I could see that Wayne's dads, his brothers, Choppinwood, and the priest had already found their places around the casket - I don't think they could see me. As for the holy man, I have a feeling he was strong-armed into attending the inhumation. His face couldn't help but look pained and The Rite of Committal was greatly abbreviated. He must have been mortified at what transpired within the walls of his church.

I almost fell asleep standing up as I listened to him recite some standard lines of scripture. His words murmured along pleasantly - like water in a nearby brook - and the sun crept toward the horizon. He said the Patron-Saint-of-Hare-Brained-Schemes' soul would soon be delivered "from the bond of sin" and his remains were ready to be reclaimed by our Earth. I heard some prayers, some blessings, three of four amens, and witnessed Wayne's family - Choppinwood included - cross themselves multiple times.

The good man of the cloth then said farewell to Wayne - for the tenth or so time - and that we're all due to rendezvous some sunny day at "a mansion in the sky." There was a moment of silence and Wayne's casket was lowered into the ground. When it hit bottom - four feet below - the priest sprinkled some Needles tap water onto it. Gary, Nick, Stefan, Serge, Jean, Yann, Gervais, and Choppinwood bowed their heads. Finally, the priest ended everything with a common burial phrase.

"Ashes to ashes," he said. "Dust to dust."

With these words, everyone promptly dispersed and I was left alone, in the somber stillness, as if nothing happened.

Since I had experienced more than enough of Wayne's family, I elected to opt out of any post-burial activities. Instead, I took an unnecessary, circuitous route to the other side of the cemetery. As there can be particular providence when one follows the steps taken once before, I soon found myself walking down Ivy Path and standing in front of vault 574. Naturally, I sat down next to it. I needed to relax and sort through all of the thoughts that had collected in my half-weary head.

It took some time for my eyes to adjust, but, after a minute or two, the reliable weeping beech trees appeared below me. Then, the small pond that lives under their branches followed suit and came into view. This time, though, the beech trees were leafless and the previously guarded gravestones were completely exposed. My eyes zeroed in on them and I reminisced about my former girlfriend. Then, I thought about Wayne and his nagging questions and comments about her. It crossed my mind, once again, that he may have known more about her disappearance from my life than he chose to acknowledge.

While I pondered this puzzle, my eyes glazed over and I fell into a fuzzy funk. At some point, though - perhaps after five minutes or so - the faint outline of a figure emerged from beneath the beech trees. At first, I thought some kind of sepulchral seraph intended to shine some heavenly light upon the many mysteries bottled up in my head. But then, when I realized that idea was completely insane, I thought there was a chance my lost girlfriend was slowly developing before me. It also crossed my mind that I was seconds away from the resurrection of Wayne – the one and the only.

Alas, none of my visions came true. The shadowy traveler turned out to be Philip, Wayne's protégé, his faithful messenger and servant. The young lad was dressed up in a little, slim cut and tailored, egg-shell blue suit. When he moved within a couple of feet of my person, he presented me with yet another envelope from Wayne.

I attempted to engage in small-talk with the youngster.

"Philip, my friend," I said. "Good to see you again. You've got a real knack for fumbling around in shadows and shrubbery, you know. Might I ask: How are you dealing with…"

Philip turned around as I was speaking - like one of those village of the damned kids - and walked away without a word. Before I knew it, he disappeared into the dark. I haven't seen him since. At least, I don't think I have.

It was too dark to read the envelope where I was in the cemetery, so I stood up and left. As soon as I walked through the front gates, I found a street light to read Wayne's words.

The letter went as follows:

Dearest Barry,

If you've made it to this point, you've done everything I've requested of you. Good job. You may take a break now and pat yourself on the back. Quite frankly, I didn't think you'd be able to squirt the mayonnaise.

You probably want to force sick cats to shit the truth at this point, but I have one last humble request.

I want you to purchase a roadside memorial kit for me from a company in Arkansas called Roadside Remembrances (good reputation, I've read all of their reviews). This kit should include an extra-large size PVC cross and the accompanying memory plaque. Make sure the PVC cross has my name on it, as well as my birth and death dates. The memory plaque should include a photo of me hugging Choppinwood (included in this envelope) and two stanzas (also included in this envelope) I wrote when I was in the middle of a profound and creative frenzy.

Yes, you're right: There is no money in this envelope. I figured the least you could do is buy me something meaningful for my death-day. Don't forget, you've neglected the day of my birth (and my death) for a number of years.

According to my calculations, the total price of the roadside memorial kit - plus shipping and handling - should amount to sixty-nine dollars and sixty-nine cents, which I believe is a phenomenal deal.

You should probably get on this right away. From what I've read, it takes at least two weeks for delivery. If a memorial isn't added promptly to the side of a highway, people tend to forget - even someone of my stature.

Sincerely yours,
Best friends forever,
Wayne

P.S. - Remember: Every uterus grows new, silver linings.
P.P.S. - Do you ever wonder why I picked you to do all of this?

When I finished reading Wayne's annoying letter, I took a look at the picture of him and the cantankerous Choppinwood. Not surprisingly, the heart-warming photo violated every rule of basic photography. Not only were the two awkwardly centered in the middle of the dining room, Wayne was also the victim of a terrible object merger - seemingly impaled by a candle sconce in the background. On top of that, it was quite clear that Wayne held Choppinwood in his arms against its will. It was turned toward him, poised to rip his face off, and murder him. One of his family members, or more likely a tripod, did a fantastic job capturing a perfectly indecisive moment.

As for the two stanzas Wayne "wrote," I immediately recognized both of them. They were the first twelve lines of *Epitaph to a Dog*. Wayne merely re-worked the inscription just enough to include himself instead of Boatswain, the famous Newfoundland dog.

"Some people say necessity is the mother of invention, but I would argue those people have it all wrong. It's the other way around, assholes: Invention is, in fact, the *necessity* of mother. Or, perhaps even more likely, *mother* is the necessity of invention."

-WAYNE

Thoughts on the famous proverb

CHAPTER 31

Dr. Drinkwater

———

I STOPPED IN TO SEE my father the day after Wayne's burial. I guess I just wanted to check in with him and see what he thought of recent events. I could hear *Family Feud* on the television as I walked down the stairs, so I had a feeling he was home. Not surprisingly, he was there, sitting at his desk, focused on re-runs of his favorite television show. Before I made contact with him, I thought about how he might die in his chair in the basement. No one would know his fate for weeks, possibly longer.

He was slumped back, looking at the television, zoned out and weary-eyed. I had to say hello three times before I captured his attention.

His head tilted toward me and he sat up a couple of degrees.

"Huh? Oh, Barry," he said. "How are you doing there? Haven't seen you in ages. What can I do for you?"

"Nothing, really," I replied. "Have you heard the news about Wayne? There was an accident."

He blinked long and hard and opened his eyes as much as he could.

"Wayne? What do you mean, Wayne?"

"He drove into a boulder on the side of the highway. Everyone thinks he's dead. I suppose he is."

"Wayne?" he said skeptically.

"Yeah, you know. Wayne. My friend with the quintuplet brothers. His fathers are state troopers."

"Oh, right. Wayne. He always was a troubled, young bird, wasn't he?"

I could tell my father wasn't interested in Wayne's demise, so I moved to end the conversation.

"Yeah, I guess so," I said.

He, however, perked up and provided some helpful advice.

"They should check his pulse," he said. "If he doesn't have a pulse, he's probably dead."

"Yep. You're right. That's what I'll have them do."

The conversation seemed like it was over to me. I turned around and headed toward the stairs.

He called out my name the second I put my foot on the first step. He likes to talk to me when eye contact is impossible.

"Barry! Before you go!" he said, somewhat energetically. "It's already November, you know? I just realized that yesterday."

I knew where his logic was headed.

"Don't you think it's about time to close the pool?" he continued. "Seems long overdue, if you ask me."

"Yeah, you're right. It's long overdue."

"Why don't you get out there and close that pool?"

"Absolutely," I agreed. "I'll get right to it."

"Remember," he said, "fully backwash that filter. You have to remove all of the dirty diatomaceous earth from the filter."

"Of course, I wouldn't dream of doing otherwise."

I was halfway up the stairs when he conveyed some more information to me.

"You know," he added, "you can use that stuff - diatomaceous earth - for just about anything. Some diatoms can be millions of years old. It's really incredible."

"Yeah," I said. "So I've been told."

And then I headed to the pool.

"Whenever you think you've got some extra money, someone else, somewhere, has devised a plan to grab it from your hands. And that's the constant, never-ending, battle humans can't resist. The question is: How can you extract money from others and prevent them from pecking at your stash?"

-Dr. Drinkwater

CHAPTER 32

Pool Closure

———————

I GOT RIGHT TO BUSINESS when I arrived at the pool. I've closed it up for several years now, so I know the drill fairly well. My father was right, though: It was a little late in the year to wrap things up before winter. Still, that didn't make much of a difference to me. I knew I could close the pool by the end of the day - well before the arrival of freezing temperatures.

Admittedly, the closure process is probably rather dull to most people - except for those who need to do it - but a description of the undertaking is both fitting and necessary. Upon reflection, it's kind of like a ritual, a tribute, or a sacrifice to welcome winter. Each step is important - cathartic even - and brings the pool-boy closer and closer to the end. Therefore, it would be a crime to exclude how the procedure is performed. More people should know.

It's true, while closing up, some folks start to feel a little despondent that summer has come and gone. I understand that reaction, but I don't necessarily share it: I look forward to the winter. Sometimes, forced change is good.

Anyhow, I began to close the pool a little after three on an overcast, but somewhat invigorating afternoon. It was cool and brisk, in the low fifties, and fairly windy. The trees surrounding the pool shifted uncomfortably to and fro, side to side, and the leaves traveled here and there - all over the place. It was well past peak fall foliage season, so they lacked their former bright yellow, orange, and red colors. They were dried up brown-toned leaves, and they scurried and scratched - perhaps searching for drinkable water - their way along the off-white cement. Every now and then they joined together, swooped up into small cyclones.

Fortunately, most of the trees surrounding the pool are pines that remain just as green as they were throughout the summer months. Sure, they lose plenty of needles - and can be a major nuisance in terms of pool cleanliness - but the benefits far outweigh the costs. Fact is, they add color to winter and they provide me with a decent amount of privacy. Privacy, of course, is the most important requirement for pool closure. A person needs to concentrate while retiring a pool for the season. A pool caretaker shouldn't have to worry about onlookers and bullshit distractions.

Accordingly, the first step I took was to make sure there were no spies hidden amid the trees and bushes. When that task was completed to my liking, I moved on to the removal stage and carried the tables and chairs off to the shed. Then, I retrieved the thermometer, the floating chlorinator, and disconnected the ladder from the deep end. Although I probably shouldn't do so, I kept the diving board in place - I like to stand at the tip of it year-round, whenever I have the urge. As for the HMS Talbot,

I removed it from the pool and set it on the concrete. I always save its deflation and transfer to the pool-house for last.

Next, I touched up the surface of the pool with my leaf skimmer that's attached to a ten-foot aluminum pole. Due to my regular maintenance, that job was easy and allowed me to move on to the skimmer basket in no time. Sometimes, the skimmer basket contains terrifying surprises due to the number of dead animals that accumulate inside it. Luckily, though, there were no lifeless rodents or small amphibians when I extracted it - only pine needles and leaves.

A sign of good fortune.

After that, the tasks that followed involved plenty of blowing, plugging, and backwashing. Clearly, these maneuvers sound sexual in nature, but they're completely chaste when performed on a pool - unless, of course, you're some kind of sick bastard.

First, I backwashed the hell out of the filter in order to purge it of dirty diatomaceous earth. This operation - my father's favorite - only took a couple of minutes. I just watched the sight glass until the water looked clear.

Second, I checked the chlorinator for any chlorine tabs, but there were none in sight. After that, I emptied a bunch of needles, leaves, and other shit from the pump basket.

Then, it was on to my trusty air compressor. I hooked it up to the pump and turned it on immediately. The sound of the air compressor is a little loud for my taste, but it's needed to blow out the pipes - as they say. Due to the design of the pool, the skimmer blew first, so I crammed and screwed a sixteen-inch skimmer guard into the proper port. The skimmer guard is an invaluable tool and helps to prevent cracks from forming due to winter freeze-ups. That stopper of sorts will, hopefully, absorb any expansion during the cold winter months.

After I attended to the skimmer, I scanned the pool to see which of the returns needed to be plugged next. It's usually a game of chance which one will need to be dealt with first and which will follow - kind of like that Whac-A-Mole arcade machine everyone loves so much. In less than ten minutes, however, I managed to plug all of the returns in the deep end and the shallow end. Everything went according to plan - no more bubbling.

When I finished with the returns, I moved on to the heater. Many folks hire professionals when winterizing the heater, but I prefer to handle the job myself. I don't trust the handiwork of others – that's the reality – and I was screwed by a subcontractor in the past.

The first step of the heater winterization process is to drain it of any water. Thus, I unscrewed the drain valve and some water and air began to shoot out instantly. Then, I turned on the air compressor once again and blew any and all excess water from the heater. Thing is, it would be a tragedy if any water remained inside it. Unfortunately, leftover water leads to an expensive summertime repair project. Henceforth, I took my time and waited patiently until only air flowed out of the valve.

I closed the valve on the heater and quickly switched the multiport valve to backwash position. Consequently, the remaining water and air were removed from the filter through the backwash hose. And finally, all of the pipes were blown out, so I turned off the air compressor - which relaxed me instantaneously. Then, as part of a brief ceremony, I dethroned the pump and filter, disabled the timer, and turned off the circuit breaker.

Now, for the second to last major part of pool closure: the addition of chemicals to the pool. For the most part, this procedure relies upon three chemicals: several pounds of shock, winter algaecide, and rust and scale remover. These chemicals are applied one after the other and mandate that pool custodians circle the pool a final three times for the season. While I add them, I can't help but think of witches gathered around a cauldron, casting spells, and dropping ingredients into boiling water.

Anyhow, I poured the shock into a large bucket of pool water - a sub-cauldron - and stirred it with a broom until it completely dissolved. Once the shock melted, I slowly walked around the pool and carefully dumped the solution into the water. Next, I walked around the pool again and applied algaecide. Then, I circled a third and final time and introduced the rust and scale remover. Lastly, I topped off those ingredients by tossing in a good old chemical ball, which will release much needed chemicals throughout the winter.

The last significant winterization step is the most difficult for me: covering the pool. Typically, the application of a pool cover requires a two-person team, but I prefer to do it myself. It's true: I've almost lost my mind applying the cover with just my own two hands, but I like to keep to myself throughout the closure process. Amazingly, this year I was able to cover the pool in record time. I utilized a secret method - for the solitary pool closer - that I refuse to disclose.

With the pool suitably concealed, I returned to the HMS Talbot and used the pump to deflate it. I carefully folded it up, put it underneath my arm, and took it with me to the diving board. I walked to the very end of the board and looked out upon my work. It was a bit dark - twilight already - but I could see enough. The water was hidden beneath the cover, the pool was free of clutter on all sides, and I felt calm and composed. Everything was organized and clean. The pool was in hibernation, asleep for the winter.

Clearly, I was tired after all of this work, so I headed to the pool-house to rest for the evening. When I got to the door I saw yet another white envelope peeking out from under the doormat. I grabbed it, opened the door, and entered my place. I flipped the light switch and saw my name written on it - **BARRY** - in bold, capital letters. I ripped it open and came across the following notification:

REJECTION LETTER

Dear Barry Drinkwater,

Thank you for your interest in the position of Courtroom Abstract Artist via Mi*rr*o Enterprises.

We received a multitude of applications for the opening, and, as such, were forced to make some *very* difficult decisions.

As you can probably guess, we are unable to offer you employment at this time. We regret to inform you that a better, more qualified candidate has been hired to fill the void.

Please consider applying for another position in the future.

We also recommend that you seek employment at a company with lower standards.

Sincerely yours,

Viola Robbins
Mi*rr*o Enterprises
"Seeing *you* in *our* reflection - since 1963."

I crumpled up the rejection letter and threw it in the trash. I knew Viola Robbins wasn't a fan of mine and this correspondence simply cemented that fact. I did wonder - quite momentarily - who received the job instead of me, but I put that thought out of mind. That's exactly what Viola wanted me to dwell on, and I didn't want to be part of her head games anymore.

I went straight to my room and collapsed in bed. The sleepy feeling arrived quickly, but was interrupted by a frightening thought that entered my head at warp speed. I lurched upward into sitting position. I had to see if I was truly alone, if Barrie was there - sitting on top of the bookcase, staring at me from across the room.

He, however, was absent. His usual space on the bookcase, empty.

I still wasn't satisfied, though, so I got up and searched around the room for him. I didn't want him to be unaccounted for - especially after his somewhat recent hostile behavior. Still, after a thorough search, he was nowhere to be found. I wondered if he ever planned to return. I wasn't sure, so I checked the closet to see if his miniature suitcase and bindle were there.

They weren't.

Barrie must have hit the road for good.

Despite the fact that he attempted to murder me with two butter knives, I have to admit I felt a little concerned for his well-being. Hitchhiking and riding the rails is a dangerous endeavor for anyone – never mind a guy of his size and stature.

"I wish my recurring dreams would recur more frequently. I need more time in them to make a difference, help the people that inhabit them, improve their society as a whole."

-WAYNE

Shipping, Handling, and Thirty-Three B

———— ◆ ————

I ORDERED WAYNE'S PVC CROSS and accompanying memorial plaque two weeks after his burial at Needles Cemetery. The memorial kit took a month to arrive, and with shipping and handling included, cost me two-hundred and sixty dollars - a cool one-hundred and ninety more than Wayne's questionable mathematics foretold.

It was the third Monday or Tuesday in December when I took the PVC cross and plaque with me and traveled to **Exit Thirty-Three B**. It was a cold day, devoid of wind and freezing in temperature - the type of weather I enjoy the most. I'm not particularly skilled when it comes to the installation of roadside memorials, but I think I did a decent job. Luckily, the ground wasn't frozen, so it was easier to complete my task than I had anticipated.

When I finished my handiwork, I stepped back to admire the fruits of my brief labor. I have to say, I was really impressed with myself. There's no doubt that I erected the best looking roadside memorial for at least twenty-five miles in either direction. Of course, I was especially happy with the epitaph I edited to better capture the essence of Wayne. It went as follows:

Epitaph to Wayne

In Front of this PVC Cross,
Beneath Your Feet,
There Lies Most of the Charred Remains
of
Wayne.
A Man Known for
Talking without Thinking,
Shaking Hands without Strength,
Trying on Swim-Trunks without Wearing Underwear,
And Several Other Vices of Man
Without His Virtues.
These observations, which are Random, but Accurate,
are Simply an Honest Testimonial as to the Character
of
Wayne,
a
Self-described Scholar and Gentleman,
Who was Born in Needles
And Died in Needles -
In an Incredible Burst of
Flame.

"The credenza - especially one with built in radio and record player - is easily the best piece of furniture ever introduced to the United States. It's of Polish origin, I believe, and is affiliated with the wife of Duke Gyula Wolk II, a woman obsessed with the act of credenza. You know, when a servant taste tests food or drink for the masters of the house."

-WAYNE

Exit Thirty-Three B: Final Inspection

AFTER I SPENT A SUITABLE amount of time basking in the glory of the PVC cross, it dawned on me that I was standing on the side of a highway with nothing left to do. I became quite aware of the cars at my back, whizzing and whooshing this way and that, traveling onward in opposite directions. It was beginning to flurry and darkness was slowly setting in, so I actually considered calling it a day. Somehow or other, the sun managed to disappear before I had the chance to appropriately acknowledge its presence.

However, as I am decidedly fond of adventuring in the late afternoon gloom - a time when everything appears more appealing and mysterious - I elected to investigate **Thirty-Three B**'s circular forest once more. It seemed foolish to neglect the convenience and the opportunity. And within a minute or two - as a matter of course - I found myself stepping across the litter-lined perimeter, headed toward whatever was waiting for me. At first, the cars zooming on the highway sounded like waves gently crashing at the beach. Before long, though, I couldn't hear them at all.

Perhaps it was the crisp air and the time of year, but there was an unmistakable vibe, an alluring aura, floating amongst the evergreens. True, most would have thought it was too chilly and bleak, but I felt alive and rejuvenated - as if my body had been jump-started with the perfect amount of electricity. All of it - the soft orange needles at my feet, the smell of the pines, and the maze of trees - left me in awe and eager to find something, anything, that could match my towering, but nondescript expectations.

I walked and walked and walked. I wasn't concerned that night had fallen outside of the forest - there was enough light to see what I had to see and I knew that I had to keep going. I probably passed some of the same trees repeatedly, but it didn't matter. Sure, it may seem illogical, but I felt that I was making progress, getting somewhere.

Finally, I saw it - something fairy floss-like, some type of sugar-cotton-wool - appear and quickly disappear behind a cluster of trees and down a slope in the earth. I tried to hide my excitement and did my best to discreetly approach the plush and the downy. I was afraid I'd create too much of a spectacle and scare whatever it was away. But I didn't. Below me, in an orange-needle-covered-bowl in the ground, I discovered a collection of magical, wayward sheep. There were two dozen or so happily running in random directions without a care in the world. Never mind one climbing a tree, I saw three, maybe four, blissfully navigating - hopping - from branch to branch.

Just like Wayne, I felt exceedingly happy. There was really something to witnessing feral, but cordial animals enjoying themselves so happily and unabashedly. Unlike Wayne, though, I didn't run down the side of the bowl toward them - I thought it best to leave them be, uninterrupted.

I stood there for a long time and watched the sheep bop, prance, and whirl to and fro, back and forth. Some even leap-frogged over each other. However, I moved on after I got my fill - too much of a good thing can be dangerous. Don't get me wrong: I greatly enjoyed and respected the sight, but I knew there was more to discover. I also wanted to leave with the thought that what I witnessed could continue, and, hopefully, never end.

I walked along the ridge of that mild glacial depression until I came upon a cryptic-looking stone arrangement. Disintegrating columns and granite slabs stood before me and were organized in a faint, queer pattern - similar to what Wayne once described. Eventually, I stumbled upon a gigantic granite head. It was resting on its side, half-smiling, as if the earth had just whispered a secret to it - some message that was previously assumed, but, nonetheless, required confirmation.

I was standing there looking at the face, thinking about the weird shit that went on - or goes on - near these eerie stones, when a voice from behind traveled up my spine and made me jump.

"I don't use that Japanese lotion to stroke it every night," the wavering and raspy voice said. "I have really dry skin."

I turned and saw an old man about thirty feet away from me. He had a long, white beard and a thin and scraggly body. Fittingly, the ancient gentleman was leaning on a cane. It looked like it was fashioned out of an antique shotgun.

"What?" I said, quizzically.

"You're the presumptuous young man who invaded my home, aren't you?"

"Yeah, I guess I am."

"Well," he said, "I'd shoot you right here and now - if I were the murdering type and my gun-cane wasn't so rusted."

We maintained our distance from one another and I continued the conversation after a brief, but noticeable lull.

"You must be Sylvanus A. Mosherbutts," I shouted into the cold air. My voice echoed and gradually faded away.

The old man appeared a bit miffed, but answered compassionately.

"The name's Sylvanus, all right - but I'm no A. Mosher Butts. As far as I know, he's the chap who invented Scrabble."

"Listen, son," he continued, "we could go on shooting the shit, as they say, but don't you think it's about time you walk off over yonder - in that direction there?"

He pointed off in the distance toward a yellow-white glimmer, dimmed by the pine trees.

I nodded my head, said "I guess so," and abided by his advice.

He didn't follow. Although I didn't look back, I'm certain he watched me until I vanished from his sight.

While I walked among the trees the glimmer turned into a glow, and, soon enough, I came upon a colossal beech, which was perfectly centered in the middle of a clearing. The tree, without a doubt, was something to behold and discharged jack-o-lantern, will-o'-the-wisp light beams in every direction. I walked to within a foot of it and studied the initials, the names, and the words carved into its bark. I touched them with my fingers and moved my hand along the beech tree's smooth surface.

I backed up to see the tree in its entirety once more, but did so as carefully as possible - I knew there was a good chance that something would cause me to trip, fall, and injure myself. I got down on my hands and knees and painstakingly inspected the ground in search of a traffic sign. It only took me a minute or two to find it and what rested beneath: a door, parallel to the earth, with a lock wheel on it - the water-tight type found on ships.

Without a second thought, I began to turn the wheel. Like an impatient toddler, I had to know what was on the other side and I couldn't pause a second for anything. With an unusual amount of energy, I spun it and kept at it until I heard a click. The door fell into place and I could turn it no more.

It was damn heavy, but I managed to open it. When I did, though, a monstrous gush of air instantly spewed out of it and knocked me off my feet. I landed on my back with my arms and legs extended, as if I was in the middle of making a snow angel on the ground. Undeterred, I got back up and gazed down into the abyss. All I could see - as my hair flowed wildly in the wind - was an iron ladder that led downward into darkness and desolation.

That's when I heard it.

It started as a soft and mellifluous tone at first - sweet and smoothly flowing. Then, it was over-powered by what sounded like a massive orchestra warming up before a symphony. The violins, violas, cellos, and double basses became one - presumably tuned to A for Abomination. They gradually increased in volume and intensity and produced a sound full of grace and power. The last thing I heard - stirring underneath the potent stringed instruments - reminded me of a train slowly rumbling, braking, and pulling into a subway station. The monstrous sound was accompanied by a high-pitched and drawn-out metallic screech - the highlight of a crescendo performance, inching toward but never reaching the end.

"I'm not really sure what happened. I'm not even sure what didn't happen. I guess it's possible nothing transpired at all."

-BARRY DRINKWATER

The CATNAP ©
(The Cambridge Aberrant Temperament Nihilist Aptitude Program)

To the Respondent:

I am about to administer the **CATNAP,** which was developed to assess character and intelligence.

When the **CATNAP** is complete, we will know more about you, your promise in life, and if you'll be a good fit here at Mirro Enterprises.

The **CATNAP** is divided into at least three sections. Your performance will determine how many sections you are subjected to, as well as the length of the testing period.

Please: Try to focus on the *here* and the *now*.

To the respondent:

The first section of the **CATNAP** involves word pronunciation. I will show you a flashcard with a word on it and you will then pronounce said word. Please pronounce each word as if you're having a conversation with a friend of equal social status. Take your time and enunciate clearly.

Please pronounce the following words:

1. Irreverent
2. Miniature
3. Orange
4. Route
5. Vase
6. Aunt
7. Leisure
8. Banal
9. Inquiry
10. Lever
11. Library
12. Irregardless
13. Neither
14. Gyro
15. Tiramisu
16. Often
17. Neanderthal
18. Salmon

19. Data
20. Uranus
21. Mayonnaise
22. Barbed
23. Applicable
24. Scallops
25. Syrup

To the respondent:

You have now completed the first section of the **CATNAP**. Good job. You may take a two-minute break to relax and collect your thoughts.

To the respondent:

Okay, the two-minute break has come to an **end.**

I am now going to ask you a series of **YES, NO,** or **I'M NOT SURE** questions. Please articulate your thoughts to the best of your ability. Avoid rambling.

The **YES, NO,** or **I'M NOT SURE** portion of the **CATNAP** begins **now.**

Yes--No--I'm Not Sure. Have you ever visited an office park and encountered a used condom lying on an asphalt walkway?

If "yes," what was the first thought that entered your mind upon this discovery?

If "no," please indicate whether or not you have ever been to an office park.

If "I'm not sure," please explain why you aren't certain.

Respondent *MUST* select one of the above options and explain his/her answer.

Yes--No--I'm Not Sure. Have you ever claimed to be the descendant of a passenger (*not a crew member*) who came to the "New World" aboard the Mayflower?

If "yes," please indicate which passenger and how often you claim to be a descendant.

If "no," please indicate if you have *any* notable ancestors who were "important" at one time.

If "I'm not sure," please explain why you aren't certain.

Respondent *MUST* select one of the above options and explain his/her answer.

Yes--No--I'm Not Sure. Have you ever dressed up in colonial garb and impersonated a historical figure?

If "yes," please indicate which historical figure and your reason for impersonating.

If "no," please indicate why you have thus far opted out of impersonating historical figures.

If "I'm not sure," please explain why you aren't sure.

Respondent *MUST* select one of the above options and explain his/her answer.

Yes--No--I'm Not Sure. Have you ever spent time exercising on a rowing machine while at a fitness center?

If "yes," how often do you imagine you are a coxswain in charge of your imaginary crew's speed and safety?

If "no," how often, if ever, do you work out and what are your preferred exercise machines?

If "I'm not sure," please explain why you aren't certain.

Respondent *MUST* select one of the above options and explain his/her answer.

Yes--No--I'm Not Sure. Have you ever fed a cat dog food or a dog cat food?

If "yes," what happened to the animal and why did you do it?

If "no," would you consider doing so in the future?

If "I'm not sure," please explain why you aren't certain.

Respondent *MUST* select one of the above options and explain his/her answer.

Yes--No--I'm Not sure. Have you ever eaten soup while standing under a tree on a cold day in the rain?

If "yes," what type of soup was it and is that your favorite soup?

If "no," can you envision yourself doing so?

If "I'm not sure," please explain why you aren't certain.

Respondent *MUST* select one of the above options and explain his/her answer.

Yes--No--I'm Not Sure. Have you ever ironed a shirt or pair of pants while still wearing either item?

If "yes," how often do you do so?

If "no," what is your standard method of ironing clothing?

If "I'm not sure," please explain why you aren't certain.

Respondent *MUST* select one of the above options and explain his/her answer.

Yes--No--I'm Not Sure. Have you ever heard a person say the phrase "stranger danger" and realized he or she was referring to you?

If "yes," how often do people say that phrase around you?

If "no," do you think that means you're considered non-threatening?

If "I'm not sure," please explain why you aren't certain.

Respondent *MUST* select one of the above options and explain his/her answer.

To the respondent:

You have now completed the second section of the **CATNAP**. Good job. You may take a one-minute break to relax and collect your thoughts.

To the respondent:

Okay, the one-minute break has come to an **end**.

I am now going to ask you a series of **HOW OFTEN** questions. Please articulate your thoughts to the best of your ability. Avoid rambling.

The **HOW OFTEN** portion of the **CATNAP** begins **now.**

How often do you inspect the structural integrity of man-made creations? For example: a dog house, a friend's living room, a parking garage, or various post-and-lintel systems.

- A. Several times a day – I'm obsessed with structural integrity.
- B. Once a week.
- C. Once a month.
- D. Once a year.
- E. Once every ten years.
- F. Never – I refuse to worry about structural integrity.

Respondent may provide a custom answer, but the above suggestions must be provided first.

How often do you check the thermostat at other people's homes?

A. Every time I'm in a home that does not belong to me.

B. Not every time, but almost every time - whenever I have the opportunity.

C. Half the time I'm in a home that does not belong to me.

D. I have, but on rare occasions when I'm bored with social interaction.

E. I have never checked the thermostat in another person's home.

Respondent *MUST* select one of the above options.

How often do you tell people about items you were going to buy for them, but, ultimately, did not purchase?

    A. As often as I possibly can.
    B. Daily.
    C. Maybe once a week.
    D. Once every two weeks.
    E. Once a month.
    F. Once a year.
    G. Never.

Respondent *MUST* select one of the above options.

How often do you tell your friends, acquaintances, or colleagues a story you've already told them - even after your friends tell you they've heard your story previously?

    A. Every time I see my friends, acquaintances, or colleagues.
    B. Several times a day.
    C. Several times a week.
    D. Once a week.
    E. Once a month.
    F. A handful of times a year.
    G. Never.

Respondent *MUST* select one of the above options.

How often do you look at other people's menus instead of your own menu?

    A. Every time I'm at a restaurant.
    B. Maybe half the time I'm at a restaurant.
    C. I always keep my eyes to my own menu.
    D. I don't go out to eat, so I don't have that problem.

Respondent *MUST* select one of the above options.

To the respondent:

You have now completed the third section of the **CATNAP.** Good job. You may take a one-minute break to relax and collect your thoughts.

To the respondent:

Okay, the one-minute break has come to an **end**.

I am now going to ask you a series of **ARE YOU MORE LIKELY TO** questions. Please articulate your thoughts to the best of your ability. Avoid rambling.

The **ARE YOU MORE LIKELY TO** portion of the **CATNAP** begins **now.**

Are you more likely to:

Clip your fingernails (forearms and hands extended outside of the vehicle) while sitting in your car at a public parking lot?

OR:

Clip your fingernails while operating your vehicle at speeds in excess of forty-five miles per hour?

Respondent *MUST* select one of the above options and explain his/her answer.

You need to travel from one floor to another and you select the escalator as your mode of transportation. Are you more likely to:

Stand in the middle of the escalator step and remain still until you've arrived at your desired floor?

Stand to the right of the escalator step and remain still until you've arrived at your desired floor?

OR:

Walk, as if you're on a regular flight of stairs, until you've arrived at your desired floor?

Respondent *MUST* select one of the above options and explain his/her answer.

Upon encountering a placid water body, are you more likely to:

Take the opportunity to skip a somewhat flat stone over the water?

OR:

Leave the surface of the water undisturbed and whistle a melancholy tune?

Respondent *MUST* select one of the above options and explain his/her answer.

You're shopping with your significant other at a high-end boutique known for its mildly scandalous, provocatively attired mannequins. While you're perusing the merchandise, you notice that your companion has become obsessed with one of the mannequins and is overtly analyzing its shapely assets. Are you more likely to:

Take issue and ask some rather pointed questions as to why an inanimate object is so desirable?

OR:

Say nothing because it's absurd to be jealous and/or care about the above mentioned behavior?

Respondent *MUST* select one of the above options and explain his/her answer.

Your significant other realizes his/her preoccupation with the mannequin has not gone unnoticed and says to you, "What can I say? I appreciate beauty in all forms."

Does this rhetorical question and accompanying answer alter your response to the previous question?

Explain.

A portly gentleman is sitting at a bar with both of his hands comfortably resting in the pockets of his navy-blue, velvet pants. On the counter in front of him is what you assume to be his drink, a cosmopolitan, also known as a "Cosmo." On the chair next to him - the only chair not occupied by a human being - is his maroon velour jacket. Are you more likely to:

Ask the man to remove his jacket so you can sit in its place?

Give up your hopes of sitting at the bar and retreat to a less desirable area of the restaurant?

OR:

Sit down at the seat - despite the fact that his worn-out jacket adorns the bar stool?

Respondent *MUST* select one of the above options and explain his/her answer.

Are you more likely to:

Mow your backyard with a lawn mower in the middle of the night?

OR:

Trim your front lawn during the day with a pair of rusty, stainless steel scissors?

Are you more likely to:

Tell the person with whom you are dining that he or she has food dangling on his or her face?

OR:

Mind your own business, keep your mouth shut, and continue eating?

It's the wee hours of the morning and you're having trouble sleeping. You're a guest at a friend's house, you're restless, and you feel hungry and a bit queasy at the same time. Because you don't want to rouse your friend from slumber, you decide to search through the refrigerator without permission. You find the following leftovers:

A. Crab Rangoon
B. Wilted Kale
C. Chicken Divan Casserole
D. One Corner Slice of Sicilian Pizza (with pepperoni and sausage)

Which are you more likely to eat? Please explain your answer.

If there were no social consequences or biological ramifications for your offspring, would you be more likely to marry a sibling of your preferred sexual persuasion?

    A. Yes, absolutely. That would be great.
    B. Yeah, I guess.
    C. I suppose - if I were forced to do so.
    D. No thanks - that's disturbing.
    E. No, way. Absolutely not. Never.

To the respondent:

You have now completed the fourth section of the **CATNAP**. Good job. You may take a two-minute break to relax and collect your thoughts.

To the respondent:

Okay, the two-minute break has come to an **end**.

I am now going to ask you a **MATCHING** question. Please provide the best answers possible.

The **MATCHING** portion of the **CATNAP** begins **now**.

Your nieces and nephews have four pets. You have not seen your nieces and nephews in a long time, so, as a surprise, you decide to purchase a gift for each pet. Regrettably, while wrapping the presents, you discover that you cannot remember which name fits with which pet. Since you respect each pet's unique identity, you must try your best to pair each pet with his or her appropriate name. The possible names are: Red-Light-Green-Light, Chutney, Packages, and Poverty. The pets are as follows: a dog, a cat, a rabbit, and a parrot. Now, please indicate, to the best of your ability, which pet you would pair with each name.

Red-Light-Green-Light   _____
Chutney   _____
Packages   _____
Poverty   _____

For bonus points: Please identify and write down gender next to each of your answers.

To the respondent:

You have now completed the fifth section of the **CATNAP**. Good job. You may take a one-minute break to relax and collect your thoughts.

To the respondent:

Okay, the one-minute break has come to an **end**.

I am now going to ask you several **MISCELLANEOUS** questions. Please provide the best answers possible.

The **MISCELLANEOUS** portion of the **CATNAP** begins **now**.

If you were asked to design a contemporary, avant-garde (not modern) style sink, what would your design be and how would it operate? Please use a piece of scratch paper and a number two pencil to illustrate your design.

In your estimation, how many people in New Jersey are named Anthony, go by the nickname Tony, and have friends who call them RigaTony?

I have just dropped a golden Parker fountain pen on the carpet. As you can see, the pen is equidistant from both you and myself. Which of the following should happen?

A. I should pick it up, as I am responsible for dropping it.
B. You should pick it up, as you are inherently subservient in this particular scenario.
C. Neither of us should pick it up, as that task is specifically reserved for office boys.

To the respondent:

You have now completed the sixth section of the **CATNAP**. Good job. You may take a one-minute break to relax and collect your thoughts.

To the respondent:

Okay, the one-minute break has come to an **end**.

You have now reached the **CHOOSE YOUR OWN ESSAY** portion of the test. There are three essay prompts below. Please select one and provide the best answer possible within ten minutes. Spelling, grammar, and punctuation count.

The **CATNAP** clock starts now.

Essay 1.

You're at a late afternoon open house and decide to investigate a large closet that's located in a roomy-second-floor bedroom. Since you're tired and no one is watching you at the time, you step behind a wall of suit jackets and comfortably situate your body between some luggage, a hat box, and three fluffy bath towels. After only two minutes, you fall victim to the sandman's peculiar handiwork, and end up sleeping well-beyond the conclusion of the open house. Not surprisingly, when you wake up from your nap, you realize the homeowners have come home. Although you're quite groggy, you think you can hear them eating carrots and hummus as they watch television in the family room.

What do you do next? In other words, what's the best way to extricate yourself from this situation?

Essay 2.

You've just met with your lawyer to discuss changes to your Last Will and Testament. When you exit the building where his or her office is located, you have no choice but to pass through a relatively small, but quaint revolving door. Unfortunately, just as you step into a vacant quarter of the revolving door, someone sneaks into the same section and you narrowly avoid injury. From this point forward, your departure from the lobby becomes unnecessarily complicated and uncomfortable. In addition, there are numerous personal space violations that make you feel disrespected and ashamed of yourself.

In your essay, please discuss the following questions:

What type of person enters the same small section of a revolving door?

Why would someone enter the same revolving door compartment?

Did the person in question accidentally or intentionally violate your personal space?

How should one address the above scenario - during and after?

What steps can be taken to prevent a similar revolving-door-rendezvous from occurring in the future?

Essay 3.

You're waiting at a train station, alone, sitting, gazing downward, half-asleep. After "who knows how long," you look up and see someone less than ten feet away from you. You then say to yourself "That person looks like a real asshole!" Seconds later, you realize that you were actually looking at your own reflection in a nearby mirror.

In a well-constructed essay, please comment upon the aforementioned event.

Consider the following:

Was this just a mistake that means nothing?

Are you really an asshole?

Is everyone else an asshole?

How do you perceive yourself?

To the respondent:

Okay, your ten minutes has come to an **end**.

You have now completed the **CHOOSE YOUR OWN ESSAY** portion of the test. You will not be subjected to any further questions.

Thank you.

We hope you enjoyed the **CATNAP** ©

Acknowledgments

———

THANK YOU TO L. CARON, D. and C. Luther, W. D. Little, P. Orzech, J. Flynn, K. Caruso, M. O'Brien (Guitar Man), and R. W. Emerson (Thoreau's eulogy).

www.ingramcontent.com/pod-product-compliance
Lightning Source LLC
Chambersburg PA
CBHW020958120726
47905CB00009B/2745